I0557799

Black Love

CHERYL BARTON

Published by: CRBarton Productions

This book is a work of fiction and any references or similarities to actual events, real people, living or dead, or to real places, are intended to give the novel a sense of reality. Any similarities in names, characters, places and incidents is entirely coincidental.

All rights reserved. No part of this publication may be reproduced, distributed, or transmitted in any form or by any means, including photocopying, recording, or other electronic or mechanical methods, without the prior written permission of the publisher, except in the case of brief quotations embodied in critical reviews and certain other noncommercial uses permitted by copyright law.

For permission requests, write to the publisher, addressed "Attention: Permissions Coordinator," at the address below.

CRBarton Productions, LLC
Email : prez@crbarton.com
Website: www.crbarton.com

Ordering Information:
Quantity sales. Special discounts are available on quantity purchases by corporations, associations, and others. For details, contact the publisher at the address above.

Orders by U.S. trade bookstores and wholesalers.
Please contact prez@crbarton.com
Copyright © 2017 Cheryl Barton
ISBN: 978-1-948-950-04-6
All rights reserved.

~DEDICATION~

To all those who appreciate real love, this one's for you.

1

"Riley, it's your mother. I know you're in there because your car is in the driveway and not in the garage. If you really wanted to avoid people, you should have parked it out of sight. You can't use the excuse that you weren't home when I stopped by and I've told you before that it's not nice to ignore your mother. Riley? Do you hear me? Leaving it in the driveway is a dead giveaway that you're home, darling, so open up."

Riley slouched down on her sofa beneath her pink fluffy blanket and held her pink and white pillows over each one of her ears, hoping to drown out the sound of her mother screaming at her from the other side of her front door. She knew that there wasn't another mother in the world like Dana Cooper and there was no doubt she would not be ignored. Still, she was hoping for a different outcome this one time. She loved her mother more than anything, but if there was one thing her mother hated, it was not being able to reach her only daughter, especially when she knew there was a crisis.

Just when the ringing of her doorbell ended, the incessant knocking started making her ears vibrate in frustration. All she wanted was a few days to herself.

Unless she wanted her mother to stand outside of her door going between ringing and knocking, Riley knew she was going to have to open the door. In her current mood, that wasn't her first preference, but she had to make some kind of move. She knew leaving her car in the driveway had been a bad idea, but she hadn't been in the most common sensed focused mindset over the past few days. Knowing her plan to hibernate for a few days, she should have moved it. If no one else came by to check on her after five days of no contact, she knew her mother would. She huffed and sat up on the chair, still not getting up. Turning toward the door, she hoped her mother would get the idea if she let on that she was okay and she could go back home.

"Mom, you don't have to be here. I'm fine and I promise you I don't plan on doing anything crazy," she hollered at the closed door, knowing her mother would be pinned close enough to it to hear her. She also knew she'd just made a move that would anger her mother even more, which was screaming back at her through a closed door without opening it. Riley knew she was asking for trouble.

"Riley Marie Cooper, if you don't open this door and stop talking to me through it, I'm going to pay some guys to break it down. I'm not your typical cool, calm and collect kind of mother, so open it right now and let me lay eyes on you. It's been five days of no phone calls, no visits, no texts and no emails. If you didn't want me to use all this technology to try and find you, you shouldn't have created all those accounts for me. This is your last warning!" Dana screamed.

Riley stood and moved to the big bay window knowing that a neighbor or two had to be outside snooping or peeping through their blinds at the scene her mother was making. She glanced back at her living room which looked more like a battle ground than her favorite space to lounge. For the past five days, it had become her place of escape from the memory of what happened to her, a day she hoped wouldn't live with her forever. Looking at the current mess she'd created, it was a far reach from the way the room looked a year ago when she was happier and ready to begin a new life with a man she loved and who she thought loved her just as much.

One year ago, this same room had been filled with wedding shower and wedding day gifts, even though there had been no wedding. Back then, all of the other rooms in her house were filled with boxes of her things that were ready to be moved to the new house she and her then fiancé, Roderick, were buying and moving into after they returned from their honeymoon in beautiful Aruba. Now, with her rooms unpacked the way they had been a year ago and her living room full of pizza boxes with half eaten pizza, stale French fries, bones from the chicken she'd been gulfing down for the past few days and various flavors of soda bottles, something she normally never drank, she wasn't sure she wanted anyone to see her like this. This had become her place of solitude where she sat feeling sorry for herself at the way her life had turned out. Looking down at herself, she was still wearing pajama pants and a long-sleeved top, a big change from the sexy lingerie she loved wearing at night. She wasn't feeling her sexiest these days.

As her mother began banging and leaning on her doorbell again, Riley gave up being stubborn and headed for the door. Unlocking and opening the door, she held her arm up over her eyes to shield them from the bright morning sun as an angry Dana Cooper greeted her with a scowl.

"Really, mom? It's kind of early even for you with all of this noise."

Riley let her in and closed the door after waving and smiling at one of her neighbors who had come out of his house for the show.

"Don't ignore me, especially when I show up at your house. You know who your mother is, so my behavior should not be a surprise. Why is this place so dark?" she said walking around pulling the curtains back and opening the blinds to let daylight in.

Riley shielded her eyes once again.

"I prefer to let the sun travel to the back part of my house before opening the blinds or the sun bakes me in here."

Dana looked around.

"You should be baked and so should this catastrophe you call a room. It could use a little fire if it means we could clean it out in one swoop. It's a mess in here. I won't even start with this new homeless looking fashion line you have going on," Dana gestured toward her clothing. "I knew this would happen. It's been a year Riley and it's time to let it go. I know what that day did to you and you have a right to think back on it and never forget it. What I don't want is you reliving it every year. Self-pity is not flowing through your veins, so get it together. I passed a few things down to you, but pity isn't one. Straighten up right now," Dana demanded.

Riley watched as her mother dropped her purse and began cleaning up the room.

"I can do that, mom."

Dana looked over at her.

"Really? Can you? I assumed if you could have, you would have by now. I've been calling you for days. I even went by your salon and was told you took the week off. Why are you drawing a bullseye on that day? What you should have been doing is taking a nice vacation on a beach someplace, reclaiming your life.

It's been a year and enough is enough."

Riley knew the storm that was her always-opinionated mother was going to drive through. She should have been prepared.

"I know and I was just about to call you when you showed up," she lied.

As soon as the words left her mouth, Riley knew her mother would see right through her attempt at an excuse.

Dana looked at her and sucked her teeth.

"Liar, but I'll give you that because I know what you're feeling. Roderick Armstrong should not be living in that pretty little head of yours a year later. I'm still working on my plan to bury and hide the body after I figure out a way to hurt him really bad without going to jail. I've spent many nights wide awake going over his demise in my head. More important to me than him, is you. I know you would need me and he's not worth it. He's definitely not worth the squalor I see in this room right now, so fix it!" Dana commanded.

Riley moved around the room picking up trash, forcing herself out of her slump. As much as she hated to admit it, her mother was right about Roderick; he wasn't worth it. It's not every day that a woman gets left at the altar on her wedding day, but even with that, the man who did that to her shouldn't still be a factor in her life. A year ago, a groom-less bride-to-be is exactly what happened to her and though she planned ahead of time for a way to deal with the memory of it, she was still stunned that she survived the embarrassment and humiliation.

"I hear you, mom and I'm good. I just needed a day."

"A day? Riley, it's been five days and it looks like you've been living in this room and only this room for the entire time. I count enough fast food deliveries for each day you've been cooped up in here. When did you add a television to this room? You have your laptop, both cell phones, books, food and even a mini cooler filled with water and ice. Were you preparing for the apocalypse and planning to live it out in this room?" Dana joked.

Riley sucked her teeth. "You're so dramatic," she said, now feeling bad about the state of the room. It was pretty bad.

Dana gestured showcasing the room like a game show host showing the prizes in the room.

"I'm dramatic? Look at this room! I'm serious, take a good look around this room, then take an even closer look at yourself and tell me who's the most dramatic?"

Riley looked sideways at her mother and laughed.

"If I answer honestly will you throw something at me?" she quipped.

Dana laughed, too.

"Okay, I am the queen of being dramatic, but this is a bit much. Shake it off and let's go shopping," Dana said.

"Shopping? What are we going shopping for?" Riley asked.

"Nothing and everything. Let's shop for whatever we want. Since when do we need a reason to shop? Today's shopping spree is on me or should I say, it's still on your father, Dana chuckled.

"I can't believe he's still paying you alimony after being divorced since I was in high school."

"Child, he'll be paying that money until I marry again one day. I have no plans of doing that. I like draining his pockets after the years I spent helping him build that million-dollar life he's living. I deserve it. It's not enough money for me to never work again, but it supplements my life pretty well. He would have made out better with the lump sum he could have given me, but he and his attorney weren't quick with the math on that one. He's got four more years of payments and he's done. Until then, let's spend more of his money, shall we?" Dana gibed.

Riley contemplated. She could use a day of thoughtless shopping to distract her.

"Okay, but no more shoes. I may need to build a closet in my spare bedroom to house all of the shoes I already have."

Dana waved her off. "That's ridiculous. Shoes are a woman's best friend. A single pair of shoes can bring a woman out of any mood. Did you learn anything from watching my *Sex in the City* DVDs? Carrie reminded every woman how important a pair of shoes are to our lives. Oh, I meant to tell you that Dawson called me a few times."

Dawson, Riley thought. They had history and a lot of it revolved around what happened to her that day. Despite the role he played, he had been a good friend. Like her mother, he didn't deserve being ignored either.

"He's been calling me, too and he stopped by a few times."

"I take it you didn't open the door for him either or was that treatment set aside for your dear old mother?"

Riley didn't want to feel worse than she already did, but if her mother was going to run through the list of people that she'd pushed out of her life for the past few days, her mood may never improve.

"I didn't mean to ignore you or him and I'm sorry for doing it. Dawson reminds me too much of that day and all I needed was a few days to myself without having to talk about what happened."

"He's trying to be a good friend. Looking at that gorgeous man can brighten any woman's day. You have a serious problem if you're immune to that. He's a walking god, an Adonis."

"Mother, stop it," Riley said. "I do not want to hear you talking about men and definitely not Dawson."

The last thing she needed to do was focus her

attention on the man who brought her the news a year ago that her fiancé wasn't showing up for their wedding, but instead, chose to take their honeymoon trip with the woman he was and still is involved with.

When Dawson approached her that day a year ago, he looked like he had been carrying the weight of the world on his shoulders. For the first few months afterward, he tried to be a good friend to her, but she kept him at arms-length. He had been Roderick's best friend until that day, a day that Dawson finally decided he had also had enough of Roderick's mess. She could tell that Dawson had been crushed by the job he was left to do when Roderick skipped out on his responsibility of telling his bride-to-be that he'd changed his mind about marrying her. Since then, she and Dawson had actually developed a pretty good friendship that had begun to turn into something more, surprising her. To say she was frightened of her growing feelings for him would be an understatement. She knew it wasn't a good idea to feel anything other than friendship and time and time again, she tried shaking it off.

"I will stop the minute you go and get dressed. I won't dwell on the fact that I think you and Dawson have fallen for each other. I won't even suggest that you should go with it and let it happen naturally. As your mother, I will stay as far away from your love life, per your request, as I possibly can and not say that Dawson is nothing like that schmuck you were about to marry last year. What I will say is if you need your space and want to push someone away, let it be me and not him. I will bounce back, but he may give up trying to show you how good black men really can be. Not all cheating, no good men – most are all that Dawson is wrapped up in a beautiful package. They get the short end of the stick most times due to the harm a few do, but not this one. He's one of the good guys and if you ask me, I'd say he's in love with you."

Riley spun around in awe and almost tripped over her own feet.

"Dawson Frazier is not in love with me. He's being a good friend," she said.

This time Dana sucked her teeth.

"Darling, are you so immune to a good man's charm that you can't see how smitten he is with you? If I have to point out what you have been for each other over the past six or seven months, then maybe the way I found you living in this room like some hoarder is what you should have. Go get dressed while I clean up in here. You're worse than I thought. That man is sexy dark chocolate, encased in magical hot melanin and every woman seems to spot that except for you. Misery has clouded your vision. I see we need to get some serious shopping done today and possibly an ice cream binge as well to clear up your vision. Momma's here to save the day, now get moving before you start talking down how sexy Morris Chestnut seems to get with each passing year!" Dana shouted.

"What's the matter with you with all of this sexy man talk? First Dawson, now Morris Chestnut?"

"What?" Dana uttered, sheepish and innocent like. "Are you talking about little ol' me? The day I never recognize a good-looking man again is the day you'll be mourning for me. I can't believe you're overlooking every sign Dawson throws your way that he's interested. I'm not the one with the problem, you are. We're going to do something about that which is going to start with shopping.

Riley started to respond, but didn't. She didn't have any words to counter and if she did, her mother would surely have more to point out that she'd been missing. Instead of continuing the banter back and forth, she headed up the stairs to her bedroom.

2

Riley walked into her bathroom where she disrobed and hopped in the shower with her thoughts turning to Dawson. Had she really been in denial about the feelings she knew in the back of her mind they were sharing? She knew she was feeling more drawn to him than ever before. Had she gotten so comfortable with his friendship that she ignored signs of more?

It was true that a few months after the wedding that didn't take place, she'd finally answered one of Dawson's phone calls after several attempts on his part to check on her. The few times he'd stopped by her hair salon, she ended up giving him one excuse after the other of why she didn't have time to talk to him.

As the owner of her own hair salon, if anyone wanted to track her down, that was one place they could find her since she spent more hours there each day than she spent at home. Putting Dawson off changed about six months ago when he showed up at the shop one night right before closing time and refused to leave even when she told him she would be okay closing up on her own. He told her he understood, but he wasn't leaving. As the water cascaded over her body, she smiled at the memory of him picking up a broom and sweeping the floor as her last customer left and she locked up. An hour later, they were still in her shop sitting in her office talking. There was no discussion about Roderick or what he had done. Dawson's only concern was how she was doing. She knew that he had never let go of her reaction when he had to bring her the bad news about Roderick. He tried to console her, but her anger caused her to put the blame on him, not because he'd done anything, but because in her mind, he was the one helping Roderick ruin what was to be the happiest day of her life. It took her months to not see Roderick every time she saw him.

That night at the salon, they talked and laughed about the latest movie out or some video one of them had come across on the internet. By the time the hour was up, he'd talked her into joining him for a late meal at an all-night diner where they pigged out on stacks of pancakes and omelets, a meal she could eat any time of the day or night. It turns out, breakfast was Dawson's favorite meal of the day, too. They talked even more about movies, vacation spots, shared about their childhood and their business ventures.

She knew from Roderick that Dawson owned his own construction and interior design business. He employed a staff of over thirty people and worked with several subcontractors when needed. Earlier in the year, he took on a partner who would soon be opening up a second location for their business because of the large interest in his company. She was happy to hear how successful he had become and how serious he was about his business.

Dawson was unlike Roderick who changed jobs at least twice a year, not being able to get along with anyone. One time, Roderick wanted to hone in on her business with an idea for them to become partners, opening up salons across the state. He had big dreams, but no follow-up. That should have been a red flag for her, but it wasn't. Thinking back, she should have been more in-tuned to his cheating on her, but once he proposed, she wrapped herself up in planning their wedding and not paying attention to her man straying.

After that night at the diner, she and Dawson had begun talking on the phone several times a week, enjoying an evening out together as friends having dinner or checking out a movie and taking time to get to know each other as friends. When the redesign of his new house was completed, something he had been working on for months, he gave her a tour and asked her opinion on some ideas for several of his rooms. His house was magnificent and she even picked a night to take him out to celebrate when his home was featured in a copy of Best Homes in the United States, monthly edition. Without paying attention, they were drifting into a zone that was beyond friendship.

She was no longer surprised when he showed up at her salon on the nights she worked late to be sure she got to her car safely. He was the first person she called when she had an idea to open a second location for her salon. By the next day, he'd already reached out to a friend of his who could help her scout out locations. The few that she ended up being interested in, he liked. He gave her the rundown on the renovations that she would need and offered to do the work for free because to him, that's what friends were for. Were they becoming more than friends and she'd missed it? She took his friendship for what she thought it was, but was it more? She had a habit of not paying attention to things that were plainly right in front of her face.

Two months ago, she was headed to an extravaganza hair event and Dawson didn't hesitate when she asked him to be her plus one. Everyone else going from her team was either married or dating and were going as couples, except her. That night, no one would think that they were only friends. They danced and he was very attentive to her desires and needs for the entire night.

She was shocked when he picked her up in a limousine and was dressed in a navy blue tuxedo which was perfectly coordinated with her white gown with navy blue accents. Where eyes should have been on the models that night, the women in attendance gave her looks of jealousy and then thumbs-up that she was the woman lucky enough to show up on his arm. That night, she invited him inside of her home and they talked into the wee hours of the night. When it was time for him to leave, they reached out to each other for a hug and time stopped as they focused solely on each other and what could be considered a starry, romantic night – a setting for lovers. As they took in the moment without saying any words, letting their eyes say it all, she saw something other than friendship. For a few seconds, she spotted something that looked like more than mere friendship in his eyes and wondered if her eyes spoke to him the same way. She saw what amounted to a man whose desire for her was about to lead him to throw caution to the wind and display affectionately what his eyes were conveying.

As Dawson appeared to lean down toward her, she didn't move. She was mesmerized by how handsome he looked and the want he had for her showed all over his face. Knowing it was coming, but not expecting the contact, the kiss he usually gave her on the cheek was directed at her lips instead. Before she knew what was happening, his lips touched hers and an electric charge zipped through her body, starting at the point on her lips where they connected.

His lips were enchanting as they made love to hers from first contact. Dawson didn't stop with a short friendly kiss on the lips, but he went in like a starving man. Joining him in the moment, she added as much zest to the kiss as he had. It wasn't a kiss meant to lead to the bedroom, but she knew he was leaving no doubt in her mind that he wanted more than friendship. There was nothing about that kiss that said friendship only. It shouted hot, passionate nights of never-ending ardent loving and for a moment, she wanted more.

Once the kiss ended, Dawson left her with the thought that anything more would be up to her, if and when she was ready. He didn't say a word as he returned to the limousine that had been waiting for him the entire time. Before getting in, he turned, waved and signaled he would call her. That kiss said everything he was feeling and if she were honest with herself, it spoke volumes for what she was feeling for him. After that night, she let thoughts of the kiss slip away as they went back to the friendship. The kiss was never far from her thoughts whenever she saw him, but she didn't want to dwell on it. When he didn't bring it up, she let it go. That, she knew, was her first mistake.

Her mother was right, she thought as she toweled dry. The signs were all there and as much as she wanted to fight it, she was falling for Dawson. Knowing she still carried around the fear of commitment after what Roderick had done, she also knew it wasn't fair to push Dawson away when he wanted to be the one to comfort her through this time. She should have answered his calls and opened the door when he stopped by her house. During one of his visits over the past few days, she thought she saw his shoulders slouch in defeat as he walked back to his car as she peered at him through the living room blinds. She didn't miss the moment he looked over at her car knowing she was inside and didn't want to see him. She'd hurt him and that was wrong. The world didn't need to suffer because she was having a moment. Dawson was someone wonderful in her life and she was handling him all wrong.

Walking out of the bathroom, she headed into her room to get dressed, feeling a lot better. She was looking forward to shopping and to apologizing to Dawson in hopes that he wouldn't hold the past few days against her.

"Let's go Riley!" she heard her mother scream from downstairs.

"I'm coming," she replied, throwing on a sweat suit and tossing her long hair up into a ponytail. After putting on light makeup including her signature pink lip gloss and adding jewelry which she never left the house without, she checked herself in the mirror and had to admit, she looked a lot better than she had been looking in her flannel pajamas the past few days. Her mother was right, it was time to get over her past and move on.

Going downstairs, she went in search of her cell phone and quickly tapped out Dawson's cell and sent him a text.

'Sorry I haven't been in touch. Dinner tonight, my treat?'

"I'm ready," she said as her mother came back into the room from the kitchen.

"Trash is out back and dishes are loaded and running in the dishwasher. Don't let me come by here and see you and this house looking like that again, especially over some man who isn't worth it," Dana said glancing around. "Now, this room again looks like a place for the living and not where dreams and self-esteem have gone to die!" she proclaimed.

"Again, dramatic much?" Riley said as she followed her mother out of the front door.

"I'm just getting started on you. As your mother, I want to be sure you understand how over the top I will be if I ever see you like that again – no makeup, take-out food boxes everywhere and flannel pajamas. Flannel? Really? Haven't I taught you anything? Sexy lingerie isn't just for a man. Wear it for yourself and always, always keep it sexy!" Dana chimed as she unlocked the car doors.

"I hear you mom!" Riley relented. She hated to admit when her mother was right and this time, she was on point. She hated those flannel things anyway. In the trash they would go when she got back home later, she thought.

Just as she reached the car, her phone vibrated. Reaching for it, she saw Dawson's name and read his response.

'Understand and dinner would be great. I need to set eyes on you to know for myself that you're okay. Call me later with when and where. I'm here if you need me.'

Riley sent back a smiley face emoji and then added one that showed the thumbs-up sign and smiled herself. How could she forget how much Dawson brightened each day?

"You know what? I'm ready to spend some money today and I'll call my father and thank him later," she joked.

Dana looked at her sideways, like she often did when Riley was being snarky.

"Have you heard from him?" Dana asked.

"No, not one phone call in over a month. Last I heard, he was headed out of the country or something. During our last conversation, he tried to chide me for not being nicer to his wife. I had to remind him that I'm grown and one day when he has a wife as pleasant as my mother, I may think about it. She's still angry about the money dad had to pay out for private school and then college. She claimed I chose one of the most expensive colleges in the country out of spite. Now that's someone who is overly dramatic. I can't imagine any woman counting the dollars a father spends on his daughter. He should be coming out of pocket considering after your divorce, he became an absentee father."

Riley was still harboring bad feelings about the way her father treated her after he and her mother divorced. Over the past year, she began feeling like her acceptance of Roderick and his mess was because she sought out the love and attention she never really received from her father.

"Well, at least we have his money and that makes up for his absence. Let's get our shopping on and I say we start with shoes - lots and lots of shoes!" Dana shouted as she backed out of the driveway.

"Shoes it is," Riley added. She smiled as she looked forward to the day ahead and for later in the evening when she would be able to spend time with Dawson.

After five days of no contact with him, she missed him.

3

Dawson turned the lawn mower off and spun around just as Angel pulled up to his house. If no one else stopped by his house regularly, his little sister did.

"Daw, Daw!" she shouted the moment she exited her car.

"You know I still hate that you call me that. We aren't kids anymore," he said.

"You may hate it, but you love me and that's all that matters. You actually cut your own grass?" she said sidling up to him and hugging him around the waist.

"Yes, and I have a riding mower out back to prove it. I use this smaller one for the front since there is less grass. I like to cut it myself sometimes. I also like to give the kids in the neighborhood a chance to make some money. Today, I have a few things on my mind and this gave me the chance to think things through. Besides, I didn't make it to the gym today and I needed the exercise."

Angel smirked at him and he laughed out loud.

"Please, you don't have an ounce of fat anywhere on you. You don't need to be at the gym every day. Are you still adding a personal gym to your house?" she asked.

"I am. The expansion is taking place next week. I want to have that completed before the deck is redone to add the outdoor Jacuzzi."

"I cannot wait to spend all of my time at your house enjoying that jacuzzi. I was telling some friends about it and I want to have a cookout once you have everything completed."

"Don't even think about it! What brings you by? I thought you were going to Vegas this weekend?" he asked.

"I am. I'm leaving tomorrow instead of today."

Dawson wasn't happy to hear Angel was going to Vegas, but she was an adult and he couldn't protect her all day, every day, though he tried. He loved that she didn't waste her time sitting around waiting for life to happen.

"Don't forget what I told you about gambling. Don't start it because it can be addictive. Go have fun and stay out of the casinos."

"I'm twenty-four and you're still treating me like a kid. I know all about gambling becoming an addiction. I'm going for the *Bad Boys* reunion concert. You know Diddy is a master at putting on a performance. We plan on hanging out a bit and then coming right back home on Monday. I have class first thing Monday morning. What are you doing this weekend?" she asked as they walked into the house.

"Not much. I have a few site visits and a business call or two that I need to take care of. Riley invited me out for dinner tonight, so there's that. Other than that, I'm hoping to have a quiet weekend. Next week, it's back to the grind. I don't take many weekends off, but I needed it this weekend. There will be no going into the office until Monday afternoon."

"Riley, huh? What's going on with that? You two dating now?" Angel asked.

Dawson knew the moment he said Riley's name that his sister would try and dive further and she didn't disappoint.

"Don't start, squirt. There is nothing there. I'm being a good friend, just like I am to you. She happens to need a good friend right now," he proclaimed.

"Right, it's been a year. Have you ever heard from Roderick again? I can't believe what he did to her. He's such a slithering snake."

"Yeah, well I can believe it. I'm disappointed in myself that I didn't do more to prevent it from getting to the point where he left her like that. No one deserves that treatment except maybe him. I never thought he'd actually do it, but when I think back on it, I'm not surprised. He was never good enough for Riley and it's best it happened before the wedding and not after."

"Does that mean you feel like you're the man for her?" Angel asked going straight to the kitchen to raid the refrigerator as she did on every visit. "Oh, my goodness, you finally picked up some of that mesquite turkey I love," she exclaimed sticking her head in the side to scope out the food.

Dawson watched as she grabbed everything she needed for a sandwich, bread, lettuce, tomatoes, turkey, cheese and mayonnaise. He sat back in one of the high chairs at the brown and beige marble-topped island and watched her make a hero sandwich that beat out any that a fast food joint could build.

"I don't see how someone so small can eat a sandwich that big," he said shaking his head.

"Want me to make you one? You know I show up here hungry all the time and I've been begging you to get this turkey. Don't act all surprised that this was my first stop," she said joking.

"No, I'm good. You can hand me a bottle of water, though," he said.

"I guess you are hungry, huh?" he asked as she piled layer on top of layer.

"I am and unfortunately, I don't have someone taking me out for dinner tonight. You and Riley, huh? I like the idea. I have always liked her and you know you're my favorite brother. The two of you are perfect together."

"We're not a couple and I'm your only brother,"

he quipped.

"You want to be a couple with her and don't try denying it. I see the way you look at her and I see the way she looks at you. Both of you are trying hard not to show and share how you really feel about each other. For the life of me, I don't know why. I hope you're not letting the fact that she was once engaged to Roderick stop you from showing her what a great catch you are."

"She was engaged to marry him a year ago and he and I were best friends," he explained.

"Right, the key word here being 'were'. I'm sure she's over him by now and your relationship with that tired model is over with, making you a free man. I didn't like that woman you were seeing. She was so into herself that she didn't have room in her life for anyone else. You treated her like a queen and all she wanted was for you to spend all of your money on her and fly around the country to meet her in whatever country she happened to be in. My brother is not arm candy," Angel declared.

"Let me clear that up for you fast. I am no one's arm candy and I know when and how to spend my money. Gina has her own money and didn't need any of mine. We had fun and it ended a few months ago without any hard feelings. I wish her well."

"I bet she didn't wish you well when you dropped her like a hot potato. I saw the news when people asked her about the fine ass man she'd been seen dating. The sneer she gave them said it all. She still wants you."

"Stop it, Angel," Dawson jested.

"I'm just saying. You, my brother, are one in a million and you shouldn't be wasted on someone like her, but Riley is another story. She is a class act. I made an appointment for her to do my hair next week. The last time I was there, the ladies were all asking if you were stopping by. They wanted to know all kinds of details about her relationship with you. I think she held back because I was there, but I saw a glint in her eyes that told me all I needed to know. Riley Cooper, dear brother, has the hots for you. I can see it in you and in her, but the two of you can't see it in each other. Inquiring minds want to know what's going on?"

"You don't need to know anything. Riley and I are friends and besides, she's having a hard time right now and she needs a friend, not a man pushing up on her."

"Whatever you say. All I need to know is the day the two of you finally give in to what has been building up for months and really start dating. Then I guess I'll have to call and knock before using my key to your house and barging in. I wouldn't want to be exposed to all the hotness that would probably melt the walls around this place."

Dawson shook his head at his ever-blatant baby sister.

"I tell you all the time to stop barging in. I gave you your own code and key to the house for emergencies, not to pop up at all hours of the day and night."

"Why? Are you afraid I'll get an eyeful of you and some babe bumping uglies!" Angel shouted and doubled over in laughter.

"Ugh, I've heard enough. This is one conversation I'm not going to have with my little sister. I'm going to grab a shower. Clean up when you're finished eating everything in my house. I'll be back shortly."

Dawson got up and headed for the shower with Riley on his mind. The text from her brightened his day. When the year of what happened to her came up a few days ago, he knew that she was probably going through something. He wanted to be there for her. Like he suspected, his calls, texts and pop-ups didn't garner a response from her. He didn't push and figured when she was ready, she would reach out. He wanted her to bounce back and realize what happened a year ago was the best thing that could have ever happened to her. He wanted her to know not all men were like Roderick. The love of a black man can be everything a woman needs when she's with the right one.

He never told her about the things Roderick had actually done behind her back and there were many. He also hadn't told her that he had been in love with her himself for a long time. He knew that she loved

Roderick for the man she thought he was. If she knew the truth, the end would come as a result of his interference. That's not how he wanted to gain her love and trust. She had to come to him on her own because she wanted to be with him, not because she saw him as her rescuer.

Angel was right when she accused him of having feelings for Riley. He had more than just passing feelings for her.

Once she'd started dating Roderick, he knew from the start it wouldn't turn out well. Roderick never knew how to be faithful to a woman. Riley was the best thing that ever happened to him, something Roderick never appreciated. He hadn't been a party to Roderick's foolishness, but he didn't discourage it as much as he should have. On more than one occasion, Roderick had accused him of having feelings for Riley. He never admitted it, but Roderick was right. He could see what an incredible woman Riley was.

Riley was that woman that every man wanted to love. She was beautiful, spirited and had a zest for life that let you know she loved everything about living and breathing. She loved unconditionally and had a good head on her shoulders, except when it came to Roderick. His slick talking conned a lot of women, with Riley being one of them. He'd tried being a good friend over the past few months once she finally let him back into her life.

For months after the wedding, she wouldn't speak

to him after that dreadful day. He was heartbroken when he saw how his words caused her to suffer. Thankfully, after months of putting on the pressure to let her know that he was sorry for his role in her hurt, she let him in. Since then, they'd become the best of friends. What he really wanted was more, but he was a patient man. If he had the chance to love Riley the way she deserved and the way he wanted to, he would never take her for granted like his former best friend had.

He was thrilled about their evening together. His concern for her had overshadowed the past few days, not allowing him to focus on much else other than what she was going through. If she was hurting, he didn't want her to hurt alone. If she was beating herself up as he knew she had done before, he wanted to offer up himself as her punching bag if it meant in the end, she would feel better. He wanted to be more than her friend, but if what she needed most was his friendship, he would be that and leave anything else for a time when she was ready. For now, dinner tonight was the best idea she'd had in a while and he was looking forward to engaging all of her beauty again.

4

"Dinner was delicious," Riley said as they left the restaurant.

When she initially invited him out as an apology for not acknowledging him for the past few days, she was going to suggest their favorite diner. As the day went on, she decided on Mexican food because of Dawson's love for beef, chicken and shrimp fajitas. Throughout dinner, she'd apologized profusely and though he told her it wasn't necessary, she felt like it was. They were friends and she didn't treat him that way. Only a good friend would know his favorite food. They were getting too close for her to completely shut him out like that.

Tonight, they talked, finished each other's sentences as familiarity took precedence and he filled her in on what he'd been up to for the past few days. Once they were sitting across from each other, she realized how deeply she had missed him.

Now that dinner was over far too soon, she felt better about where they were and hoped that their friendship was still on track. To where, she didn't know, but she knew she needed him in her life. She smiled up at Dawson as they walked to the parking lot.

"I'm glad you invited me out tonight. I missed seeing and talking to you," Dawson said.

After his day of one business call after another on his planned day off, they agreed to meet once her mother dropped her back off at her house.

The moment he saw her get out of her car at the restaurant as he sat at a window seat inside waiting, his heart began pounding. Never had a woman had the impact on him that Riley had. She was more than beautiful. Nothing ever stopped him in the past from having a dating life, but thoughts of Riley and what they could one day be together curtailed any desires he had for any other woman. He would be lying if he said the fact that her gorgeous body wasn't another reason he was drawn to her. She was shapely and filled out in all of the right places. While he always appreciated a beautiful woman, it was the total package that appealed to him the most.

He was all man and the first thing he noticed on any woman he was drawn to were her legs and Riley's were the legs of a statuesque model. They were powerful, toned and still all girl and sexy. He had a penchant for working out and knew that Riley was serious about her exercise game. It showed in her gorgeous body. It never mattered to him what she had on, she had a flair for fashion. Everything she wore looked like it was made exclusively for her. She kept up her beauty regiment without trying too hard. He knew she was a beauty whether she was dressed in sweats or in an evening gown. Her nails and hair were always done with perfection and to see her strut in high heels with the confidence of a woman who knows that she's got it going on, he could look at and admire her all day on any given day. As they walked he glanced over at her several times and when their glances met, he didn't look away. He wanted her to begin seeing more than just friendship when she looked up at him.

Riley turned to Dawson as they reached her car which was parked further away than his. Always the gentleman, his first thought was always about her safety and that stood out for her every time they were together. She'd never had a man go to great lengths like Dawson did at making sure she was on his mind. He openly cared about her, never letting her forget how beautiful she was to him. How could she continually miss those messages that were clearly being given to her? She thought again about her treatment of him over the past few days and felt the need to apologize again.

"I want to apologize again for not returning your calls and texts and not answering the door when you stopped by. I needed a moment, though that isn't a real excuse. I have a habit of feeling sorry for myself and I got caught up in that. I'm over that feeling now. I don't understand how I can still allow what happened back then take me to that sunken place. I'm over it now, but that doesn't erase the fact that I'm still letting that time get under my skin."

"You're human, Riley and it happens to the strongest of people. I told you there was no need to apologize to me. I understand and I hope next time, you'll reach out to a friend, even if it's not me. Don't sit in that house alone reliving a bad moment in your life alone. Sometimes you need another person to help you get through what's bringing you down. If no one else is around, I'm here for you. I want you to know that and never forget it. I hope you see that I want to be that shoulder when you need one. You've been there for me whenever I've needed to vent."

Riley hugged him around the waist and then stepped back when she felt a desire to hold him tighter and never let go.

His muscular, toned body invaded her dreams at night. Whenever they hugged, those dreams came to the forefront of her mind as they were doing now. She wondered if she was reading signs from him of more than just friendship or if she was imagining it. She'd been wrong about men before and still wasn't sure of herself when it came to men.

"Sorry about that," she said, shyly.

"Sorry about what? Hugging me? You can hug me anytime you want and if you ever need a hug, I'm here to oblige."

Dawson smiled, showing her his pearly whites and her heart melted. This man was dangerously handsome and the way he smiled made her body tingle. There was a loving yet sexually deceitful look about him that made her think of him in ways that were more than just friendly. She shook those thoughts off and focused.

"You're always here for me and I appreciate it. I've always known that, even over the past few days. It was an unnecessary, self-imposed seclusion. So, what are you getting ready to do? It's a Friday night, just after ten," she said leaning against her car.

"I didn't have any plans past us having dinner. I'll probably go home and chill. I don't get to do that often enough. I have a ton of movies I need to catch up on that I'll let watch me as I look over some paperwork for the business expansion."

Riley had been excited when he shared with her his plans to expand his fast-growing company. If anyone deserved this level of success, it was him. To her, he deserved everything that was good and wonderful in life because he was a good and wonderful person.

"Still doing that? I can't wait to hear more about the progress you're making," she said, happily.

"You'll be the first person I'll call when all the

dotted lines are signed."

Dawson stared down at her. Though she wore high-heels for their dinner, he still stood over a foot taller than her. To him, they were perfectly meshed when it came to height. Everything about her was perfect to him. He agreed that the night was still young and he wasn't ready to leave her company yet.

"I promise to answer the phone," she joked, making light of her treatment of him lately.

Dawson laughed with her and knew that her apology came from the heart. Five days of not talking or seeing her seemed like an eternity. He had time to make up for.

"Would you like to come by and keep me company? I know it's late and I don't know if you had other plans after dinner," he said hopeful.

"Sure, I'd love to. I don't have anything planned for this evening. My first thought for dinner tonight was the diner where I figured we'd sit until the middle of the night like we've done before. This place closes in an hour, so eventually they were going to kick us out. You have any snacks at your house? I'm not talking about that healthy stuff you call a snack. Trail mix and health bars are not considered a snack to anyone other than you. That's not real food unless you're a rabbit," she laughed.

"I have snacks coming out of my ears these days. If I don't buy them, Angel will stock my cabinets with them when I'm not there. The only things I don't have are peaches and cream ice cream, your favorite and caramel kettle corn, your second favorite. I'll stop on the way to pick those up and you can meet me at the house." Dawson reached for his phone and sent her a text. "I just texted you the code to get in. You don't need a key. I also sent you the code to the alarm on the wall as soon as you walk in. If you get there before me, make yourself at home," he said.

Riley smiled up at him.

"Are you sure? I could follow you to the store and then to your house," she said.

"I'm sure. I trust you and feel free to snoop. There is nothing there to find," he joked.

"You mean I won't find any panties stuffed in the cushions or sexy lingerie from some woman who hid it away to scare off any potentials you may have over?"

Riley said it in a joking manner, but hoped his answer was that there was no such woman like that she needed to worry about.

"Trust me, there are no signs of any other woman other than Angel at my house. If you'd like to leave a piece of lingerie at my house, feel free to stop at home and grab some and hide them before I get there. That, I wouldn't mind at all," he said and reached for her car door to open it for her. "Get to my house safely and I'll see you in a few. If you think of any other snacks you want me to pick up, text it to me while I'm at the store."

In his mind, it was time to change the subject to

anything but Riley and lingerie. He knew it was a dangerous topic the minute the words left his mouth. A picture of her in something hot and sexy was the last thing he needed at the moment.

"You're too good to me, Dawson Frazier. I'm lucky to have you in my life," she admitted.

"I hope so," he said after she got in and closed the door. He waited for her to leave the parking lot before jogging to his own car. Jumping in, he headed in the opposite direction in order to grab ice cream and a few other snacks like popcorn and chips, things he knew she liked. Whatever she wanted, he would be all over it if it meant she smiled every day. He never got enough of seeing her blissfully happy knowing he had a hand in it. She had no idea that he would do anything for her.

5

Dawson was wrapping up his last team meeting of the day, catching up on construction project progress while he had been away on business travel for the past week. After everyone had left and he was left alone, all he could think about was Riley and how much he'd missed her while he was away.

Since that night three months ago when they had dinner as an apology for her ignoring him during a time when she was down and depressed and then spent a fun evening at his house watching old black and white movies, hanging out had become a constant for them.

Talking to her several times during the week while he was away helped him keep his sanity over how much he missed her. He was also thankful that she graciously agreed to look in on his house and let the crew in to continue the work on his house. Usually he asked his mother or sister to look out for him, but they both happened to be out of town at the same time. Riley didn't hesitate when he asked her and she already had a code to get in and deactivate the alarm system from that night months ago when he'd given them to her. The plan was to give her the passcodes to get in that one night while he ran to the store, but he left her programmed code as they were just in case she needed to get in another time. They were getting closer. She was on his mind first thing in the morning and the last thing at night. Now that he was back, he couldn't wait to see her.

The last text he received from her was that she was planning on making it an early night at the salon after being there since four in the morning to do hair for an entire wedding party of twelve. She was going to be dead tired considering how seriously she was about giving every one of her clients the best service possible.

An idea popped in his head at how he could help alleviate the stress of her day and selfishly got to spend time with her. His plan was to invite her over, cook dinner and they could relax. It was also his way of thanking her for having his back once again. His cell phone rang interrupting his thoughts of her.

"Hey, Mom," he said answering.

"You're back in town?" she asked.

"I sure am. I got back last night around midnight. When are you and Davis coming back?" he asked.

His mother and step-father had been on vacation

out of the country where they traveled first for business Davis' law firm and then they planned on spending an extra week in Italy for some downtime.

"That's why I'm calling. We're going to stay a few extra days. I'll be back on Tuesday instead of tomorrow. Angel is coming back tomorrow from her trip with Mia. Everything at your house okay? This is the first time all three of us have been away at the same time."

Angel had taken a last minute impromptu trip with their step-sister, Mia who was two years younger than him at twenty-eight and four years older than Angel. One of the reasons behind the divorce between his parents was the fact that his father had an affair while they were married which resulted in a daughter they didn't know about until she turned ten. By then, Angel had been born and the marriage between his parents was pretty much over anyway. They divorced and his father, Ed, ended up marrying Mia's mother. It was complicated, but strangely enough, once the siblings knew about each other, there was no keeping them apart. He, Mia and Angel were close despite the animosity between their parents. His mother even embraced Mia, though she and her ex-husband were like oil and water.

"All is good at the house. Riley looked out for everything while I was gone. I was about to head over to her shop when you called," he said.

He heard a pause and knew he'd just opened the

door to a conversation about Riley.

"You know I like you with Riley. She's good or you."

"I'm not actually with Riley, mom. We're good friends," he said.

"You should be with her. What are you waiting for? Some kind of special invitation? The two of you act like you're dating, but both are afraid to acknowledge there is something between you," she said.

"Now, you sound like Angel," he said, remembering the conversation with her that sounded a lot like this one.

Dawson could hear his mother breathing loudly in frustration. What was it with the women in his family telling him how to handle his personal life? If it wasn't his mother, he was getting it from Angel and Mia equally. He wanted more from Riley, but the issue was still whether or not she was ready. He was more than ready for her, but wondered if pushing her could result in severing what they'd already built. He knew how fragile she still was when it came to trusting me. His mother may be able to provide some insight for him after what she went through with his father and how she still opened herself up to love again after the hurt.

"Mom, when you met Davis, how did you know he would be what dad didn't turn out to be for you? You were married to dad for thirteen years, but once you met and married Davis, it was like you were a new person. You were happier than we ever remember you being with dad. Even though I love my father, I love Davis equally because of how much we could see that he loved you and us. How did you know that Davis was that one for you?" he asked.

Though he'd been in love with Riley for a long time, his love for her had grown exponentially over the past few months. He wanted to express his love for her openly so bad, he ached when he let an opportunity to do so go by whenever they were together. He wanted more and he wanted to give her more. She had to sense something was going on between them because not only were neither of them dating anyone, they never talked about dating other people.

"Is this more about Riley and you than Davis and me?" she asked.

Dawson hesitated, not wanting to give too much credence to his question, but he needed to know how his mother felt once she knew she was with 'the one'. His father had been unfaithful, but she still found it in herself to love again and trust again. He wouldn't get the answers he needed if he wasn't open with her.

"Yeah, it is," he said.

"I knew it," he heard her say on the other end of the phone. He could almost picture her pumping her fist in the air with jubilance.

"You're right that I have feelings for Riley that are

beyond friendship. I've never felt like this about any woman before. I don't question whether what I feel for her is real or not because I know it is. I've also never been in love and Riley is who I would consider 'the one' for me."

He waited for her response and could practically hear her smiling through the phone.

"Well, I met Davis when I filed for divorce from your father. There was no need to drag that sinking ship out for years once we knew it was over. I love Mia like my own daughter despite the years of tension knowing she was conceived during my marriage to him and how long he was able to keep that a secret."

"Mia has always been that second sister to me and it's because you welcomed her with open arms despite what dad did," he said. Thankfully, Mia's mother and his mother thought of the children first and never kept them apart.

"Well, what your father had done was unforgiveable, but Mia didn't need to suffer because of it. We had you and Angel, who we loved very much, but the relationship went down-hill right after she was born and it quickly died once I found out about the affair. Davis was one of the lawyers at the firm where the lawyer who represented me worked. I know you've heard the saying, 'you had me at hello'? That is what happened with Davis and me. He said hello to me on an elevator and by the time it reached the ground floor, we had exchanged numbers. I think I fell in love with him the moment he said he wouldn't call me until the divorce was final. He didn't believe in seeking out a woman who was not free to be sought after, even if she's going through a divorce. I respected that and he held to that. A few days after the divorce was final, he called out of the blue and told me he'd been asking his colleague about the case. Once he was told my divorce from your father was final and all the paperwork was signed, he reached out. We were inseparable from that day forward and forever more."

"How did you get over the hurt of what dad did?" he asked.

"I have always believed in love and I didn't let what your father did keep me from believing love still existed for me. While Davis and I dated, I learned to trust again because he was patient with me. He went out of his way to prove to me that men like your father wouldn't be every man I encountered and he was right. When I let go of the hurt, I found love and it was real and wonderful. You know I always say there is nothing better in this world than black love."

"Yes, you have. That sounds like a true, fairytale love story," Dawson said.

"It was and still is. He's always treated you and Angel like his own and his kids embraced all of us from day one. He became someone I thought about before going to bed and the first thing in the morning. I smiled just thinking about him even if no one else was around. He loves me unconditionally and has shown me that kind of love from the beginning. Now, tell me what's going on?" she asked.

"You already know. I'm in love with Riley, but I've been keeping my distance and keeping things on a friendship level. It's a tricky situation considering the past, but I can't help that I'm crazy about her. I think she feels the same way about me too, but like I said, it's tricky. I think she has trust issues because of the whole Roderick situation and even after a year, she's still hesitant. I'm not sure she's ready for me to love her. I'm not sure she trusts being in love again."

"Son, love can be tricky, but if it's real, it can be wonderful. You with Riley remind me of Davis and me. She will trust and love again and I think what you are doing and how you're doing it is exactly what she needs. Keep showing her that you can be the man she always dreamed about having. You're on the right path."

"That's good to know because she means everything to me."

"Son, the times you've brought her to the house, the two of you act like an old married couple, finishing each other's sentences and already knowing what you each like to drink or what you like on your grilled burger. You started this out right by being her friend and probably one of her best friends. If you want more, tell her how you feel and don't let her get away. I think that time has come. She's already like family. Davis is calling me to hurry up. We're going out on a yacht today with some partners from his firm. I'll see you when I get back. I need at least a few minutes to call Angel and check in. I'm proud of you, Dawson. Riley is lucky to have someone who loves her as much as you love her and you are real about that love. That's important. Love you!"

"Love you, too, mom."

Hanging up, his thoughts turned back to Riley and though he knew she was probably crazy busy at the salon, he still wanted to see her.

"Emily, I'm heading out," he said to his office manager as he walked into her office. "I've read and signed all of the new contracts. Can you scan them in before you leave and send out the necessary emails with attachments?" he asked.

"Will do. I take it the business trip went well?" she asked.

"It did. I was going to brief you early next week. Right now, I want to do something that doesn't involve work. Larry and I can brief everyone next week. He was a great asset on this trip. He's going to be excited when I tell him he's being promoted now that we're expanding. He's been my right-hand through all of this," he said.

"You're going to need more staff soon with all this new business you're bringing in," Emily said.

Dawson knew the underlying issue is that Larry isn't the only person who should be up for a promotion and he was already working on that.

"I'm already taking care of that. I'm starting with getting you some extra help around here. I want you to do the interviews for two new office staff since they'll be working directly with you every day and before you ask, yes the new responsibility of overseeing the new team members will come with a hefty pay raise for you."

Dawson smiled when he heard Emily laugh behind him as he headed out the door.

"I wasn't going to ask because you are always looking out for me and I appreciate it. Are you coming back today?" she asked.

"I'm going to head over to check up on a few worksites which will tie me up for the rest of the day. I'll see you on Monday. Let's close the office for tomorrow and give everyone a Saturday to enjoy family. One day off for the company won't hurt. Have a good weekend!" he shouted back before closing the office door behind him.

6

Riley found a moment to escape and disappeared into her office for a few minutes of peace and quiet. She'd finally finished her last customer of the day and was too tired to even get in her car and go home. She'd been working since early in the morning on a wedding party for an evening ceremony. Thankfully, everyone showed up on time and she was able to get everyone out of the salon an hour earlier than scheduled. She had been invited to the wedding, but declined. She would show up at the hotel to complete the bride's hair after she had her dress on in an hour, but after that, her plan was to go home and stay in the entire weekend doing nothing, something she very seldom got the chance to do on a Saturday.

First, she needed to find the strength to clean up and then make it to her car on feet she wished she could take off, they hurt so bad. This was the life of a stylist and due to her popularity with not only permed hair, but natural and braided styles, she was always going from one client to the next without much of a break. Her aching feet were now the result of such a day.

Leaning back in her office chair, she placed her feet up on her desk and closed her eyes. On the back of her eyelids, an image of Dawson in all of his fineness appeared causing her to briefly forget about the pain in her tired feet. He had been due back from his business trip the night before. No doubt, he was playing catchup around his office and on various job sites which is why she hadn't called him yet.

She had missed him the week he was gone. She was thankful for the chance to feel close to him when she went by his house every day to check on it and take in his mail. While he was gone, he'd been sending her the sweetest text messages and if she wasn't careful, she'd be more in love with him than she already was, if that were possible. Saying the word love in her head made her sit straight up in her chair. When did that happen?

Dawson had been a great friend and they had the best time whenever they hung out and love was something that had been building up over time. To her, it was now in full bloom. In the silence of her office, that reality hit her like a bolt of lightning. Dawson was the type of man that little girls hope to grow up and fall in love with. What were they doing? Were they just hanging out? Were they dating? Something was happening and they had become so comfortable with the situation that neither had taken the time to define it.

Several times she wanted to address it, but her fear of being turned down held her back. What would she do if she showed her affection for him and he didn't feel that way in return? Is this what being distrustful of men was like? Would she ever be able to get over the hurt of feeling like she wasn't enough? Dawson was nothing like Roderick and deep down she knew that and didn't doubt it. On the surface, she feared giving too much of herself and not getting the same in return. What was happening with Dawson was deeper than friendship and that, she couldn't fight.

"Love though?" she said out loud.

"Love?"

Riley jumped when she heard Dawson's voice. She turned toward the door and there he stood looking like her everything.

"What?" she said.

"You said the word love just as I walked in."

"I did?" Riley thought she'd said it in her head.

"You did."

"That was nothing. You're back!" she exclaimed and jumped up from her chair and practically leaped into his arms. She was happy he caught her before they ended up on the floor.

"Yes, I'm back and I've missed you. Is my house still standing?" he asked the moment they drew apart, something that happened too soon for him. She was no longer in his arms, though they were now holding hands.

"It is. I'm a good house babysitter. You haven't been home yet? I thought you were coming in last night," she said.

"I did. I was joking with you. My house looked just like it did when I left. I see the men got a lot of the work done out back. I like the new higher fence. I don't want any kids getting hurt getting into my yard and taking advantage of the pool and hot tub. Thanks for letting them in for that. How have things been around here? You look exhausted."

"I am. I had that wedding party this morning and that drained all of my energy," she said.

"All of it? I was hoping I could talk you into dinner as a thank you for looking after things while I was gone. Maybe I can cook something good and you can come by, kick off your shoes and relax. I wasn't planning on much this evening after the long week away. What do you say?" he asked.

Riley quickly calculated in her head and realized they had been spending a lot of Fridays relaxing either at his house or hers. She missed him while he was gone and couldn't think of anything else she'd rather do than spend an evening with him.

"Sounds like good plan. I get a meal and I get to relax with little or no effort on my part? That's a woman's dream. Don't you know?" she joked.

"I do. Don't forget, I know you as much as you know you," Dawson said.

"I have no doubt at all. You want me to bring anything?" she asked.

"Just all that beauty and an appetite and I'll be a happy man," Dawson said. "I'll let you wrap up here. Come by whenever you're ready. I'm heading there now after picking up what I'll need for dinner. I've been out all day and I need to wash off the dust from the sites I visited today. You're not hanging around to lockup, are you?" he asked.

"No, one of the other girls will be locking up the shop tonight. I'm going to jet over to the hotel to finish the bride's hair for the wedding which shouldn't take long. I'll call when I'm on my way," she said.

"You don't have to do that. Use your code and come on in, the alarm will be off. I'll probably be in the kitchen slaving over this incredible meal I'm planning for you," he smiled.

There is goes again, she thought. There was that smile that made everything right in her world. She looked down and saw that they were still holding hands and neither made a move to drop their hands. When she looked back up at him, everything in the room seemed to fade away and there was just the two of them. The pull to him was strong and she wondered how much longer she'd be able to fight it. If only she could trust what she was feeling. She had a feeling they could be much more.

Dawson noticed the silence surrounding them as Riley looked up at him. If he weren't careful, he would take what he saw staring back at him as love, the word he heard her say when he entered her office. The need to kiss her slammed into him hard and it took every bit of energy he had to not go there. He'd done that once and though it was nice, things were awkward for a few days. Tonight, he wanted to talk about them. He loved their friendship, but he wanted to be more to her and hoped she was interested in the same thing. He didn't want to convince her that she could trust him, he wanted her to know it for herself. He wanted her to trust him with her heart and know that he would never tread on it like what had happened to her in the past. Before he took a step he wasn't sure she was ready for, instead of kissing her, he leaned down and kissed her on the cheek. That was enough for now, but he didn't intend on that being their only form of affection forever. Her salon wasn't the place to make a move.

"I'll see you tonight then," she said.

"Yes, you will."

Riley shivered and was glad they were no longer holding hands. She was sure he would have felt her reaction to him. Besides his very good looks, he had a distinctive voice which was deep, husky and yet raspy at the same time. It was smooth and oozed all kinds of sexiness that made her think of how her body would tingle if he were whispering in her ear. She could listen to the sound of his voice all day. She already knew she was a goner, yet she still fought it. Damn to what happens when you lose trust in what you're feeling. She had no one to blame but herself.

As Dawson turned to leave, she walked behind him to her office door and watched all the women swoon over him as he greeted and acknowledge each one of them before he left. Once he was outside of the salon, everyone turned to her and gave her the thumbs up as if they knew something was going on between them that she wasn't aware of.

"You are so lucky to have a man like that interested in you," one client said in her direction.

"Yes! All that glorious sexiness in one strong, vigorous package. I could look into those dreamy eyes all day long and that smile!" another patron said.

Riley smiled without giving a response. She also didn't deny anything was going on with him. It's what she wanted, but didn't know how to let go and get it. She gave them all a smile and a wave and disappeared back into the quietness of her office.

Alone again, she collapsed back into her chair and the excitement of spending an evening with him was all she wanted to focus on. Even with tired feet, she could do a dance she was so thrilled. She sat back in her chair, spun it around with enthusiasm and smile with glee like she'd just won the lottery.

"Would the two of you just do it already?"

Riley stopped spinning when the receptionist

walked into her office. Kimberly had been with her since the beginning when she first opened her shop six years ago and they'd become not just boss and employee, but friends.

"What are you talking about?" she said, feigning ignorance to the comment.

"Riley, you are the only person who hasn't acknowledged your love for that sexy ass man. You know you want him and I hope and pray that the reason you are hesitant has nothing to do with that clown you were about to marry. Dawson is nothing like that and that man is in love with you. You are also madly in love with him, so do it already."

"What makes you think I'm in love with him or that he's in love with me? Has he said something?" she asked.

"Of course not, but unless you're blind, it's obvious. It was obvious to every client in the salon just now and I see it every time he shows up here. Your own persona changes when he's around. I see the difference in you whenever you talk about him. It's taken a lot for you to feel this way about a man again. My hope is that you don't let him get away because of a past hurt. That is one fine, chocolate specimen and you know there is nothing better than to be on the receiving end of black love from a man who only has eyes for you."

"He is something special," she said.

"Damn right he is and you would be a fool to

continue to act like he's just a friend. Some woman will snatch up all that yumminess right from under your eyes. There isn't a woman alive who wouldn't do that man in a second, but he's not the player type of guy. He wouldn't use a woman like that. He wants you and only you."

"And I want him," she admitted. It was the first time she'd said it out loud to anyone.

"Trust what you're feeling and not what your reservations are," Kimberly said.

"I'm trying to."

"Go with it girl and don't focus on what has been in the past, but on what could be a loving future for you. Now, get out of here before you're the cause of that wedding starting late. Any plans after that?" she asked.

Riley looked up at her and knew she was making reference to Dawson.

"Yeah. I'm having dinner at Dawson's house."

"Yes, and get you some because you my sister, are overdue!"

Riley sat with her mouth opened as if she was going to say something to counter what Kimberly had just said. Knowing she was right, there was no need to. She closed her mouth and sat stoic before exhaling.

She watched Kimberly retreat and packed her things to head to the hotel. She was going to do her best by trusting her feelings and praying that past hurt didn't interfere.

7

Dawson heard the chimes ring throughout the house signaling the opening of the front door. He had been home for a few hours and after running in and grabbing a quick shower, he was now in the kitchen with the oven on and pots cooking on the stove.

"Dawson?" he heard Riley call out.

"I'm in the kitchen!" He walked out to greet her just as she was removing her shoes to place them in the box he sat by the door. He smiled at the thought of how well she knew him. He loved preserving his floors and she knew he never walked around in shoes. "Hey you!" he said walking up to her.

"Hey, yourself. This place is smelling good and until I walked in the door and the food hit my nose, I didn't realize how hungry I was. My stomach is already growling," Riley said.

"Well, you won't have to wait much longer. I have vegetables steaming on the top of the stove and my famous lasagna from scratch is in the oven along with my famous twice-baked potatoes."

"I have never met a man who loves to cook as much as you do. You should have been a chef. Where did you learn to cook meals from scratch? I think your baked macaroni and cheese is the best I've ever had," she said.

"My mother was serious that I know how to take care of myself once I moved away from home, especially after my first year away at college when I moved into an apartment with some friends. He didn't want me starving and hated wasting money on fast-food all the time. She taught me all of her recipes."

"Ah, the smell of fresh garlic is music to my nose," Riley said as they walked back toward the kitchen. "Thanks for the invitation. I'm sure I would have gone home and filled up on snacks and no real food. No one cooks when they're as tired as I am. I surprised you're not too tired to cook after your long week away," she said.

"I am tired, but I was more excited to see you and spend time with you tonight. Knowing that I would see you and cook for you, I had energy I didn't realize I could must up. I'm glad you didn't change your mind and go home to crash."

"And miss a Friday night hanging with you? Never!" she exclaimed. "Is there anything I can do?" she asked.

"You could make us a salad. You'll find all of the fixings on the bottom shelf."

Riley washed her hands and jumped into action. She got what she needed from refrigerator and when she turned around, Dawson had already placed a bowl on the counter.

"Tell me about your trip," she said as they worked together on dinner.

"Well, I met with the representatives from the firm who are planning on building a new private middle and high school here in Phoenix. They want to contract with my firm to build it. I'm looking over the specifics in order to prepare a few ideas for the design. This will be a nine hundred seat school with state of the art learning, arts and sports environments that will become a model for other schools that will be built around the country. It's a forty million-dollar project, all funded by a private donor who left the money with specific instructions that it be used to build a school. The firm representing the client's estate chose me from recommendations from other clients, one being a lawyer at my step-father's firm that I constructed a multi-million-dollar home for. They are looking for a structure that will be powered by solar energy, a place where children will love to come and learn."

"Wow, that's amazing! I'm excited for you."

"Thanks. It is exciting. In my mind, I already have a completed structure in my head. I'll start getting those ideas to my team next week to prepare us for the presentation that's taking place in two months. While

I was in Chicago, I picked up a little something for you," Dawson said before reaching for a bag that he'd sat on the kitchen table. He handed it to Riley as she gleamed from ear to ear.

"You bought me a gift?" Riley exclaimed.

"I did and it's not a gift to say thank you for house sitting for me, it's a gift to let you know I thought about you while I was gone. When I saw this, I thought of you," he explained.

Riley took the bag and removed the purple and white paper from inside. Underneath sat a long box. She opened it and inside was a beautiful Pandora bracelet with several charms."

"It's beautiful," she said looking over the charms individually.

"I hope they aren't ones you already have. I know you like those bracelets, as a lot of women do."

"I don't have any of these already," she said touching one charm after the other.

Looking at them, she was familiar with the Pandora collection and knew that each one of the charms that Dawson had selected were about friendship.

"I'm glad. I want this one to be very special and as our friendship grows, I'd like to add more charms that I find that speak to what I'm thinking when I think of you."

Riley was stunned into silence. She removed the bracelet from the box and reached it out to him to put on her wrist. After it was in place, she continued staring at it. Nothing has or ever would be more special to her than this moment and this bracelet she now wore on her left wrist. She already had two Pandora bracelets on her other wrist, but this one, she wanted to be sure sat special and separate by itself because it was one of a kind.

"I don't know what to say. I love it. This is more special to me than any other piece of jewelry I own. I know that sounds a little cliché, but it's the truth. I wish I could find the words to tell you what this really means. Perhaps by the end of the night, I will," she said, almost on the brink of tears.

Dawson was overwhelmed with joy. The moment he thought about her while walking through a shopping center, he happened to be standing outside of a jewelry store. When he told the woman behind the counter that he had a special friend he wanted to purchase a gift for, she began showing him various items. The moment he saw the gold Pandora charms, he knew what he wanted to get. This way, he could build on it based on the direction their relationship went in. He was hoping to go from buying her charms about friendship to buying her charms that signified love.

"I'm glad you like it," he said.

"I love it," she replied. Riley walked over to him and gave him a hug to thank him and before she knew it, her lips were pressing against his. The moment he drew her closer to him, she felt enveloped in a cocoon of love. His embrace was tight and his kiss was electric. Though the fact that they were kissing surprised her, she went with it.

Dawson didn't know how they went from talking to kissing like two loved-starved people. He never second guessed what they were doing, but loved the fact that she appeared to be enjoying the kiss as much as he was. He gave her all of him in the kiss.

Lifting her arms up, Riley held on to his shoulders as he plundered her mouth of everything he needed, giving her exactly what she needed and wanted from him. She heard a moan which drove her more to give as much and as good as she was getting. This was Dawson, she thought as the kiss went on and on. This was the man she'd been dreaming about at night and oftentimes, unable to get to sleep as thoughts of being in his arms like this raced through her mind, not allowing it to rest for slumber. Was that her moan or was it Dawson? She didn't know because she was floating on a cloud of desire as he made love to her mouth. No man had ever taken such care in kissing her like this before. She felt on the verge of passing out she was so over-awed with exhilaration.

Just as she reached to pull him even closer, the timer on the oven went off, surprising them both. They drew apart when the chime shook them back into reality.

She didn't move and neither did Dawson as she

reached up and ran her finger across her lips where his lips had just been caressing her into submission. Neither of them took their eyes off of each other as the impact of what they'd just shared crossed between them. Riley didn't know what to say. Looking at Dawson, he appeared just as stunned as her at how good kissing between them was. They had kissed once before a while back, but that didn't compare to what they'd just shared. This was more intense and went a lot deeper than two friends sharing a moment. This was so much more.

"I better get the lasagna out," Dawson said, breaking the hypnotic trance they were in.

Riley cleared her throat and stepped back. She initiated the kiss, but Dawson had taken it to another level. She couldn't quite read how he felt about it. He turned into a willing participant, but she didn't know if it started out that way. Did he do it to oblige her? Riley shook off the thought. She had to stop second-guessing a man's reaction to her. Dawson was genuine. Why couldn't she just go with that?

"I'll finish the salad," she said turning away and walking back to the counter. They worked together in silence and after several moments, they started to speak at the same time. They looked at each other and laughed. Just like that, the awkwardness was gone.

"You first," Dawson said.

"How about you first this time?" she said. "Whenever we do that, you always let me go first."

"Okay, then I'll go first this time. I know this is a terrible moment to ask this considering the kiss we just shared, but are you seeing anyone? Dating someone?" he asked, not looking up from checking the pot on the stove.

"No, I'm not seeing anyone. When I'm not at the salon or hanging with my mother, the only other person I've been spending my time with is you. I haven't had time to date or see anyone."

"Do you want to spend your time with someone else?" he asked.

Riley responded without any hesitation.

"No."

"Are you almost finished with the salad? I'm going to get plates out and we can eat. Everything is done. We can eat here at the counter if that's okay with you. If you prefer, we can eat in front of the television," Dawson said.

He mumbled on trying to figure out what to say next. He wanted to jump for joy that she wasn't seeing anyone and excitement flowed through him that she didn't want to see anyone. She may not have admitted she wanted to see him for more than just friendship, but it was a start.

"I know you're not going to leave the conversation like that," she said.

After grabbing plates from the cabinet, Dawson sat them down and then leaned back on the counter next to the stove and turned, giving her his full attention.

"I have more I want to ask, but I don't want to get too much into your personal life."

"Since when are there questions that we can't ask each other?" she asked.

"What were you going to say to me?" Dawson asked.

"We really are two peas in a pod. I was going to ask you about your personal life. Ever since that night a few months ago when we hung out here after dinner, we've been doing that a lot, like three or four times a month. I know I don't have any kind of relationship or dating life right now as I just told you, but what about you? There isn't a woman who would want more of your time on a Friday night? You are an incredible guy and know I'm not the only woman around who knows that. Are you hiding a woman I don't about? I don't picture you as the playboy type, so I won't assume you have women in and out of here on some kind of schedule. I hope I'm not prying. That was some kiss we just shared and I think it begs for a conversation about what's happening, don't you think?" she asked.

Dawson could hear his heart beating loudly in his chest. They were having the talk or the beginning of the talk about what was going on between them. Neither were dating, yet spending all of their time together like two people dating. They had to stop straddling the fence.

"I'm not seeing anyone at the moment. I was

seeing someone several months ago, but that ended. Since then, like you, I've been knee-deep in work, family time and enjoying times that I get to spend with you."

"Some people would say we're in some sort of relationship, but you and I are the only one's not acknowledging it. Are we in some sort of relationship?" she asked.

"I want us to be, more than I want to take my next breath. What I don't know is how you would feel about that?"

Riley stood quiet, unsure of what to say next. What she was feeling for him wasn't one-sided. She didn't know what to say. She had no time to digest what was happening. As much as she'd like to answer his question, she wasn't ready as doubt plagued her once again. Breaking eye contact, she picked up the salad bowl and moved it to the spot where they would be eating.

"The salad's done. Do you need help with anything else?" she asked as she thought about his loaded question.

Dawson turned back to the stove realizing she was deflecting and to him, that was okay. He wanted her to think about what he asked and decide if she wanted more between them. He didn't want to put her on the spot.

"No, I'm good. Let's eat," he said.

8

"What is it with you and these black and white movies?" Riley asked as Dawson took the remote from her and turned to the channel that played old movies all day and night.

After eating dinner where they talked about everything except for the question he'd asked her, they retreated to his favorite room to get comfortable and finally relax. The kiss, hovering over them like the floating elephant in the room wasn't far from her mind. She sat at the end of the sofa with her feet up across his lap where he'd placed them as soon as they sat down. For the past twenty minutes as they watched television together, he massaged her feet and she luxuriated in letting him. On his own, he remembered her saying how tired and achy her feet were and as soon as the opportunity presented itself, he reached for her feet. His fingers and hands were magical and any minute, she was imagining herself falling asleep. The pain in her feet was officially gone.

"I love old movies. My mother always had them on the television when I was growing up and I've been unable to shake my love for them. You don't like them? This relationship is over because my black and white movies are a make or break situation," he joked.

"Relationship?" she asked.

He looked over at her and saw a seriousness that he knew needed to be addressed. No longer interested in putting off the discussion anymore, he turned the television off. He wanted to have this talk and neither of them were going to run from it.

"What do you think we're doing, Riley?" he asked. "I know we didn't continue our talk over dinner, but it's not going away and neither am I," he admitted.

She exhaled and looked him in the eyes the moment he turned to her.

"I don't know," she said.

"I do and I'm not afraid to admit what I think it is."

"Okay, enlighten me," she said curiously. She knew she had doubt in herself, but Dawson didn't carry that trait. He was surer of himself than any man she'd ever met.

"As long as you promise not to run for the hills, I'll share," he said smiling.

"Not running, so share."

"I know we're not in a relationship other than a really good friendship, but a relationship is what I want with you. I said it before dinner and I meant it then. Wait, that's not exactly true. Let me start over with some real truth. I love you, Riley and not just as a friend. I'm in love with you and I have been for quite some time – longer than I really want to admit at this point. I have enjoyed the true friendship that we've developed. If there was ever a woman that I would want to love, it would be a woman that I have the kind of friendship with that you and I have. The best and greatest love starts with a friendship like ours. What you do with this information is totally up to you, but I want you to know that I haven't been seeing anyone else because I've been waiting on you to be ready for me."

Riley's heart was racing. She heard the words coming out of his mouth and couldn't believe the man she was secretly in love with just declared his love for her.

Sliding forward on the chair until she now sat on his lap where her feet had been, Riley didn't reply with words, she replied with a powerful kiss that she hoped showed him more than she could tell him about the love she felt for him. Though she had no doubt what she was feeling for him, doubt did settle in when it came to openly stating her feelings. Before long, the kiss turned wild and she knew that as much as he wanted her, she wanted him equally.

As the kiss grew hotter she reached down and caressed his chest through his shirt and all she wanted was to feel his skin. This was Dawson whose arms she was in, whose lips she was touching with her own. She wanted to feel his skin against her skin. She wanted the moment she dreamed about now that she knew that the love she felt for him wasn't one sided.

"Off," she said. "Shirt, off!" she demanded. "I need to feel you. I've been waiting to hear that you want more than friendship with me and now all I can think about is being close to you."

"Are you sure?" he asked, breathlessly.

Without words, she kissed him deeply again. Knowing he had his answer, she felt him move to give her what she wanted.

Dawson pulled his shirt up and over his head without breaking eye contact. Once it was off and he felt her hands against his bare chest, his body hardened like never before. The moment he knew that Riley felt his hardness rise under her behind, he knew there was no turning back. He had the woman of his dreams in his arms, right where he wanted her to be. He wasn't expecting it tonight, but he wasn't one to look a gift horse in the mouth. As much as he has wanted and desired her, he would give her anything she wanted at this point.

"You feel amazing in my arms," he uttered against her lips as he nibbled around them.

"You feel incredible," Riley said and rejoined her lips with his in a dueling match of tongues, taking them to their own private heaven.

"Should I stop?" Dawson asked as he kissed a path across her chin and down around her neck.

"No," she whispered. "Make love to me."

Dawson leaned back and looked into her lustful gaze.

"Are you sure? I mean, I know how much I want you, but are you ready for that?" he asked.

"Yes," she whispered.

Dawson held her tighter against him as he trailed open-mouthed kissed further down her neck to the exposed area on her chest, licking a wet path across the flesh of her cleavage.

"I've wanted you like this for a long time, sweetness. I'm afraid to move in case this is a dream and any movement may cause me to wake up," he admitted.

Riley leaned back and to help prove what they were doing was not a dream, she placed an open-mouth kiss on the center of his chest before kissing a track across his pecs. When she did, Dawson shifted beneath her.

He couldn't stand the temptation any longer. Standing with her in his arms, he headed for the steps that led up to his bedroom, kissing her all the way, letting her know how much he appreciated the fact that she wanted him as much as he wanted her.

Rushing up the stairs, he walked with her over to the bed where they continued devouring each other. As the kissing went on, Dawson began exploring her body and touching all the places that he'd always wanted to introduce himself to.

"Hurry!" she said, impatiently. "I need you."

Standing, Dawson removed the rest of his clothes.

Riley watched him undress and her pulse quickened the moment he lowered the zipper on his jeans and freed himself. She shifted around anxiously on the bed imagining what his size would feel like inside of her. Nothing prepared her for what her eyes had laid upon. He was much larger than any visual she'd had of him in her dreams. She watched as he reached for a condom in his nightstand and kept her eyes on his hardness as he sheathed himself before rejoining her on the bed. She had been so focused on watching Dawson's every move that she hadn't removed her own clothing. With shaky fingers, she began unbuttoning her shirt as Dawson reached for her.

"Let me," he said.

With a lot of love infused in his blood for her, he painstakingly removed her clothing one piece at a time.

After sliding her lace and silk panties down her long, luscious legs, Dawson kissed his way back up, starting at her calves, getting to know every inch of her. When he reached her knees, he took a little bite causing her to jump, knowing the feeling shot right to that spot between her legs, adding to her readiness for him.

As he kissed his way further up her body, he let his fingers probe her womanhood, sliding his fingers around her lower lips, rejoicing at how much the essence from within her body seeped out, coating his fingers. She was more than ready for him. He loved how turned on she was for him. The feeling and desire matched his for her.

"I can't wait much longer," Riley pleaded, not only with her words, but with the way her body began writhing around on the bed in anticipation of him going deep inside of her, finally joining their bodies.

Her eyes followed his as he made his way all the way up her body, stopping along the way to kiss and tantalize her overheated and over-sensitive exposed skins. The moment she watched his mouth open and close around her pebbled nipple, she felt like any minute her body would shoot straight up from the bed. She felt like she'd been waiting a long time to be loved the way Dawson was doing and now, as much as she wanted to draw the moment out, all she wanted was to feel. She wanted to feel him enter her body as her gaze held his while he loved her. She wanted to feel her body reach its climax while he held her lovingly in his arms. She wanted more of his kisses that drove her body from zero to sixty with the first touch. She wanted more of Dawson and from the look in his eyes, she wasn't alone.

Coming up to a position in between her legs, Dawson leaned down and took her lips in a kiss fueled by his love, desire and thankfulness that she was choosing him. He wanted her to know that he was staking claim on her on this night. He wanted her to be where he was; where he had been for a long time. Now that he was here, he wanted to carry it out as long as possible, but need overtook him. With the fingers on one hand, he parted her entrance and now positioned where he wanted to be, he slid inside of her body, stealing his own breath the moment he felt her warmness on the hard, chiseled head of him. Pulling himself partially back out of her body, he slowly worked himself in and out, allowing her body to get accustomed to his size.

Dawson had to grind his teeth using all of his might to not thrust harder into her, to get all the way inside. Her tightness caused him to take his time.

"You feel so good," Riley groaned out as she joined him in a grinding motion he started the moment he entered her.

"You're going to kill me," he whispered as he leaned down, going between kissing her lips and kissing around her neck.

The moment she felt Dawson go all the way inside of her, Riley released a breath she'd been holding in as she concentrated on the feel of him. She'd never felt so full, so complete before and the way Dawson began working inside of her, she could already feel her climax within reach, much sooner than she wanted. The anticipation of being with him had her on the brink before any clothes were even removed.

Dawson thrust harder and deeper, panting and feeling like a wild animal in heat. The way he felt encased in Riley's body was confirmation that this is where he was supposed to be, rising higher and higher feeling out of control. He wanted to be free and he wanted her freely flying high with him.

Riley fought hard to keep her orgasm at bay as her legs trembled uncontrollably, but that was a losing battle the way Dawson was making her feel. Her body instinctively increased its thrusts, matching Dawson as he increased his surges into her. Before long, they screamed together with passionate howls as they came in mutual gratification riding the wave of ecstasy together. Riley could feel her body floating as one pleasured feeling after another shot to all parts of her body.

Dawson didn't stop moving, and couldn't if she wanted to, even after her breathing returned to normal. She held onto him until his body's wracking subsided with his own orgasm.

Riley knew this wasn't just sex between them, this was love and though it felt good, it also scared her. Her feelings for Dawson ran deep, but she'd been there before. She loved being in his arms and she felt miserable that she was unable to share with him the fact that though she loved him too, she was afraid of her feelings for him. Self-doubt was winning again and she didn't know how to fight it and get what she wanted. What she really wanted to do was tell him how much she loved him, too. Self-doubt made her remain silent as she held him tight in her arms as he whispered words of love for her over and over. She silently cried inner tears that she had a loving man in her arms who she knew loved her unconditionally and yet, she still held a part of herself away from him. Past hurt was a beast on new love, she thought and held him even tighter.

9

Riley woke up, dazed and feeling like she'd just had the deepest sleep of her life. Slowly becoming aware of her surroundings, she remembered she was at Dawson's house. She wasn't just at his house, she was in his bed and she was naked. She felt her body cocooned against Dawson while he spooned with his arm draped across her body, lightly snoring in her ear. She was afraid to move as she stared at the wall across from the bed. The passionate activities from the night before came to her remembrance and her heart started beating furiously in her chest at the thought of what they had done together. She remembered the night like it was still happening. When she moved slightly, the ache between her legs reminded her even more. She'd made love with Dawson and not just once They'd made love more times than she could count and a sign of that were the numerous number of condom rappers that were strewn about on the nightstand next to the bed. What he remembered the most was never getting enough of him.

Dawson had pleasured her in ways that were foreign to her until coming together with him. He was an unselfish lover who time and time again, sought to bring her pleasure first as she begged him to do so again and again. Throughout the night, she couldn't get enough of him, wanting him more and more after each explosive completion. The moment she thought her body was too exhausted to rise to his lovemaking, she didn't hesitate to jump at the chance to feel him inside of her again and again.

Her body shivered slightly at the feeling of the moment he slipped his head between her legs and drove her wild. She thrashed about looking for anything to get a grip on to control her body that had developed a mind of its own – a mind that wanted more and more of Dawson as the night went on.

Now in the light of the early morning, she was questioning herself for what she'd done as once again, doubt set in. Why couldn't she allow herself to feel and forget about reservations when it came to men or at least this man in particular. He wouldn't hurt her, cheat or deceive her. They spent the night together, moving into a realm that was more than friendship. Dawson had become that person she had come to count on and though she loved him, she was afraid she'd put their friendship at risk especially knowing that she was afraid of love, even of loving Dawson.

Riley turned and looked over at him sleeping soundly and wondered if they'd made a bad move, letting their desire for each other overshadow common sense. They had a history that would hover over them, easier to deal with as friends and much harder to move beyond now that they'd been intimate. Thinking about the consequences of what they'd done, she felt closed in, unable to breathe. She needed to go home. It was hard to think with a naked and clearly hard Dawson lying in bed close against her. Her traitorous body wanted him as much as her heart loved him. It was her mind that was defiant and wouldn't let her give her all, even now. She hated herself for not being able to embrace what they could now have.

Slipping out of Dawson's embrace, Riley slid out of bed, careful not to wake him and looked around the dimly lit room for her clothes. She quietly slipped into them as quickly as she could, keeping an eye on Dawson the whole time, praying he wouldn't wake up knowing the discussion she didn't want to have would take place. She wasn't ready to face herself, wondering if rejection from Dawson would be down the road.

Knowing her shoes and purse were downstairs, she walked toward the bedroom door when she spotted some papers and a pen. Grabbing them, she jotted down a quick note to let him know she was sorry, but she had to leave. She couldn't stay and look him in the face. What they had done was a mistake and she was sorry if it ruined their friendship. Leaving the note on the bed, she tiptoed down the stairs, remembering to deactivate the alarm with the code he'd given her. Quickly slipping on her shoes and grabbing her bag, tears formed in her eyes as she made haste getting to her car. She wondered if she would ever be able to let herself freely love again. If she couldn't give her heart over to Dawson, the finest man she'd ever met, what did that say for her hope for a future of love. She only had herself to blame and kick around because Dawson had done everything right. It was her. She was a lost cause. Maybe she didn't deserve someone as great as him.

Experiencing the longest ride home of her life, Riley didn't know what to do as she drove home with tears streaming down her face. She loved Dawson so much, but couldn't bring herself to love him. It didn't make sense to her and she knew it wouldn't to him either which is why she left without waking him. She couldn't face him. She had a hard time facing herself. Her heart raced, she couldn't focus and she worried that she'd just ruined the best friendship she'd ever had. What now, she thought. What else would she allow a time in her life a year ago that crushed her to impact her ability to move on to bigger, better and great things?

"Damn you for what you did to me!" she shouted and banged hard on the steering wheel. She wanted to blame Roderick, but she first had to blame herself for not being able to let of the bad and walk openly into better.

~~

Dawson stretched as he slowly woke to find that he was in bed alone. He expected to wake up to Riley being in his arms. The night before was everything he thought it would be. They made love like their bodies had already known each other as they came together in perfect sync. He had never made love to a woman who responded to him the way Riley had. She was as hot for him as he was for her and not just the first time, but every time he reached for her or she reached for him. Sitting up, daylight poured through the slits in the curtains, but the room was still pretty dark. He listened for any sound and heard none.

"Riley?" he called out and listened for her response. Getting up out of the bed he slipped on the jeans he'd dropped on the floor the night before and with a prickly feeling across his skin, he went to the bedroom window and looked out over the front of his house. Something told him he would not see Riley's car in the driveway where she'd parked it the night before. His hopes of waking up to her were dashed the moment he saw an empty spot and realized, she'd left.

Going back toward the bed, he saw what looked like a piece of paper on the bed. Picking it up, he read the note she'd left explaining how the night before was a mistake. He read her attempt at trying to explain herself, but what he took from it was that they'd made a mistake sleeping together and now in the light of day, she couldn't handle it.

"Damn!" he said angrily. He wasn't expecting that. They'd made love like they were excited to finally get to that point after walking around it for months. Their connection had been there for a long time and the night before, they'd finally faced what they were feeling or at least he had. Riley clearly wasn't sure by the fact that she disappeared like a thief in the night. He didn't know what time she'd left, only that he woke up happy that they'd crossed a barrier only to find that they were possibly further away than they were before. Reaching for the phone on his nightstand since his cell phone was still downstairs, he dialed her cell phone and hoped she'd answer. She had a habit of not wanting to face what bothered her, but he was determined to not let her walk away from him afraid of what was next for them. They had come so far and now she wanted to go backwards. He loved her too much to not let her see that his love for her was real enough for them to help her deal with her insecurities. He wasn't giving up.

He waited through two rings when she finally answered.

"Riley, what's wrong? I woke up and you weren't here. In place of you I find a note on the bed pretty much explaining to me that last night was a mistake."

"I'm sorry," she said. Riley had been home about an hour knowing that eventually he was going to call once he found her gone. "I had to get out of there."

"You didn't enjoy being with me? Making love didn't mean anything to you?" he asked.

"Don't do that. This is what I wanted to avoid, this kind of conversation. See, things have already changed for us."

"You're saying they didn't change for the better? I went into this knowing what I felt for you and making love with you only enhanced that. It didn't lead me to question whether or not doing so was a bad idea. What gives? What are your reservations?" he asked, hoping to get her to open up to him. They'd come so far and now he felt like they'd taken a few steps backward.

"It's not you and I don't want to take back what we did last night. It was wonderful, but can you say it isn't going to affect our friendship? Did we move too fast?" she asked.

"Too fast? Did you not want me the way I wanted you? After what we experienced with each other, I feel like it was damn near perfect. You can't keep running away from your heart. I'm not going to hurt you," he said and waited for a response, but none came. "You know me and you know I'm not that guy. I've wanted to be more than just a friend with you for a long time and I thought we were on the same page."

"I don't know what's wrong with me," she pouted.

"Nothing is wrong with you other than you being scared to love again. I get it. Remember I was there with you and I know what you're thinking, but don't put me in a category of men who could possibly walk all over you. You were comfortable with our growing friendship, but going into something more, you're ready to run, which you pretty much did leaving without waking me up. Leaving a note though? Come on, I deserve more than that."

"I know and I'm sorry. I don't want to lose your friendship. I can't say I'm ready for more. I enjoyed being with you. It was incredible and I've never experienced lovemaking like that before. I just need a little bit of time," she explained.

"What does that mean, you need time? Does that mean I won't hear from you or see you? Our sleeping together equates to the friendship being ruined in your eyes?" he asked.

"No, I hope not. I hope our making love hasn't ruined what we had."

Riley's thoughts were all over the place. She wanted him, but feared commitment again. She didn't want to lose him, but she didn't know how to hold on to him without doubting herself.

"Nothing is going to ruin that. I'm still here and I still want and love you, but if what you need is time to think through all of this, you do that. I know things may change, but I'm hoping that's not the case. I can't imagine not having you in my life because we crossed a line that now you're having regrets about."

"I'm sorry," she said, not knowing what else to

say.

"Don't be sorry. Think on this for me," he said. "I am Dawson Frazier, not any other guy you've ever known. I love you, I want you and I would never, ever hurt you. The way I feel about you isn't going to change because you're indecisive. I'm not going to say anything crazy like, if I can't have you the way I want you, then I don't want you at all. You have turned into one of my best friends and that will never change. Are we good on that front?" he asked.

Riley felt a little relief. The last thing she wanted to do was lose his friendship because she couldn't get her own act together. One thing she did know was that Dawson was a great guy and the issue lies within herself.

"I hear you and yes we're good. Can I call you later?" she asked.

"You never have to ask to call me. You know how to reach me just as you always have. I know you must be tired after our marathon of a night. I'm going to let you go. I'll call you later," he said.

Without waiting for Riley to respond, Dawson hung up as he questioned himself about how fragile she still was. He'd done everything to let her know she was safe with him, but he understood the hurt she endured and she had trust issues. He damned any man who didn't treat a woman with respect, honesty and love. Once he's done his damage, the issues the woman was left with became the problem of the next man. That hurt leaves a woman not knowing how to let go and live in the moment again. Heading to the shower, he needed to get out of the house and get his mind focused on something else while he hoped things hadn't in fact changed for them.

~~

Riley looked down at her cellphone which felt like lead in her hands. She didn't handle that well and she definitely didn't say the right thing. What woman does that? Who leaves the bed of a gorgeous hunk like Dawson while second guessing if the best night of intimacy that she'd ever experienced was the right thing for her? Not a woman with any common sense.

She stood stoic in her living room trying to catch her breath. What was in inside of her that wouldn't let her openly love this man back? He was doing everything right; everything a woman could ever ask for. To top it off, he did things to her body that should be recorded in books. She didn't even recognize herself with him. She was wanton, forceful when she declared what she wanted and every time he reached for her, her body and her mind were ready, willing and splendidly able. That was as close to a perfect combination for love that she could have ever longed for and yet, here she was, still denying him.

She was startled when her phone vibrated in her hand.

"Hey mom," she said answering her mother's call. She always knew when to call because Riley could use some advice.

"Hey, baby girl. I've been trying to reach you since last night. I have two friends who needed their hair done today and I was hoping you could squeeze them in."

"I'm actually off today. I was going to have a quiet day at home, but after my night last night, I need something to occupy my mind."

Riley knew she'd already said too much and her mother wouldn't be able to keep herself from digging in.

"What happened to your night and do I really want to know? You know you got your flair or drama from me," Dana laughed.

"I took a leap and then regret set in and now I've officially slid into self-pity," she admitted.

"Again? For what this time?" Don't lie to me either because I'll be able to hear it in your voice."

Riley hesitated and thought about how much to share. She and her mother were close, but the very private and intimate parts of her life, she never shared. "I got a little close with Dawson and this morning I sort of ran out on him while he was sleeping."

After admitting her wrong, she bit her fingers like a nervous child waiting for the scolding she knew her mother was about to issue all over her life.

"You did what? So, you and Dawson finally took things up a notch and you did what? Tell me you didn't tell him last night was a mistake."

Riley could hear her mother's exasperated breath on the other end, no doubt frustrated with her.

"I did that and more. I left a note telling him that very thing and now he's hurt and I don't know why I did it. I think I'm ruined for any good man to want me," Riley said right before she began to cry.

"Whoa, no crying. I know you're upset and a little angry with yourself that you can't seem to find your balance and let Dawson into your heart. What you did was wrong if deep down, you really want him to love you and you love him back. You have to let go of the past and pray that man has the patience to go through this time with you. Dry your tears and give it a few days. If he doesn't call you, you call him. Don't lose him over your own insecurities. Fight it and get your happiness back."

Riley wiped her face and calmed her crying.

"I am. You always know the right thing to say," she said.

"That's because I'm your mother and I know your heart, just as Dawson does. He may not be as hurt or angry as you think he is. Like I said, give it a few days and I believe everything will be alright. You're not planning on spending the day sulking, are you? I don't want a repeat of that."

"No. I had a busy day yesterday, but if you have some friends who need their hair done, I can meet them at the salon. I need to get out of here today and not sit around feeling sorry for myself."

"Good. I'll call them and we'll meet you at the salon. I hope you have some wine. If I'm going to spend my day there, I'm going to need a few glasses."

Riley laughed. She could always count on her mother to brighten her day.

"Yes, there is plenty of wine and a large glass just for you. I'll see you there," she said and hung up.

Her mother was right. She needed to take a little time and deal with her issues and then call Dawson and apologize.

10

"Dinner tonight was a great idea," Riley said as she sat across from Dawson at her favorite Chinese restaurant.

After three days of no contact after their night together, Dawson called her and invited her out for a bite to eat. They sat in the dimly lit restaurant enjoying her favorite dish of shrimp and broccoli over fried rice. Dawson had ordered Shrimp and Lobster sauce, his favorite and they were now enjoying after dinner drinks and talking.

"I'm glad you agreed to have dinner with me. I haven't seen you in a few days and I was missing your beautiful face," he said.

"I guess I made things a little awkward between us, something I didn't mean to do."

"It's okay, Riley. I want you to know I understand and my invitation to dinner was hopefully a sign to you that our friendship is still intact. I don't want you to drift away from me. If what you need is time, time you shall have. Are we still on for a movie after dinner?" he asked.

When Dawson asked her out to dinner and a movie, she thought he meant a movie night at his house, but he was referencing an actual movie theater. She assumed he as avoiding anything that could lead to a repeat of what happened the last time she was at his house. Going out to a movie would also prevent them from talking about that night – a night where he confessed his love for her and she didn't return the sentiment. She had time to think over the past few days and she hoped they would have some quiet time to talk about it. That didn't seem to be his plan since they wouldn't be talking in the theater.

"Yes. We should probably get going if we're going to make it on time. Do you want to follow me back to my house so that I can drop my car off? Remember we met here separately because I had a late client," she said.

"Sure, we can do that. The theater is closer to your house anyway."

"Then perhaps after, we can go to my house and talk?" she asked. Riley nervously tried to make the step toward resolving her own inner issues and what she really wanted was him. She was more than ready after realizing she hadn't had one single night of peaceful sleep since she'd left his house. That was because she was going about this all wrong. She wasn't allowing herself to be in love knowing Dawson was as close to a perfect man as any woman could find. She didn't want to fight it anymore.

"Talk?" Dawson asked.

"Yes, talk. I think it's time we really had a heart to heart about that night and about other days and nights to come. This isn't the place to do that and of course a theater isn't either. I really want us to talk, Dawson. I've missed you," she said.

"I've missed you, too. Are you sure you're ready to be in a confined space alone with me?" he joked.

Riley laughed, happy that they could laugh off the tension.

"I feel safer with you than with anyone else. I do want to see this movie as long as you agree we can sit down and talk afterward?" she said.

"Deal."

After getting the check, paying and including a large tip, Dawson stood and took Riley by the hand as they walked toward the door. Knowing that she wanted to talk about them, he felt comfortable taking her hand. If things went the way he hoped, they would be holding hands a lot more. He was grateful that they didn't lose track of the friendship they'd been enjoying and hoped that her willingness to talk meant that she was ready for more with him.

Riley walked with extra excitement because tonight, she was planning to tell Dawson that she loved him too and she was ready to go to the next level with him if he still wanted her.

As they walked hand in hand, she stopped abruptly when Dawson's grip on her hand surprisingly tightened. She didn't know what happened and looked up at him. When she saw his face, she could tell something or someone had startled him and she looked around to see what or who it was. She looked around, but not behind her and then a familiar voice shook them both.

"Well, well. What do we have here? My best friend Dawson and my fiancé. Imagine that," Roderick said standing up from his table and coming up behind them.

Riley's skin itched the moment she heard that all-too familiar voice. They had to have walked right by Roderick's table in the restaurant and Dawson must have recognized him first.

What was he doing in Phoenix, she thought? The last she'd heard, he was living someplace in California with the woman he'd left her for over a year ago. She and Dawson turned around and faced him at the same time. She had not seen him in over a year and she wasn't happy about seeing him now. She had hoped she'd never have to set eyes on him again.

"Roderick," she said. "What are you doing here?"

She watched as he looked from her to Dawson and then back to her. It was obvious he was more than shocked to see them together and holding hands like a couple.

"Well, clearly my presence is a surprise. Almost as

much of a surprise as seeing the two of you together. Are you holding hands? Again, my fiancé and my best friends out on a romantic date perhaps?" he asked.

Riley was seething at his attempt to disparage what she and Dawson were doing, which to her was none of his business. Instantaneously, all she felt was rage. Her mind went back to that day over a year ago when he'd left her to deal with a wedding that wasn't taking place and now here he stood, sneering at her. He has some nerve, she thought. She looked up at Dawson first and she could see he was about to address Roderick and she cut him off. This was her moment and she signed for Dawson to wait. She then turned her fury so that it landed squarely on Roderick.

"Let me clear something up for you real fast. I am not your fiancé. When you don't show up for your own wedding, that means you also no longer have a fiancé," she said fiercely.

Roderick held up both of his hands like he was surrendering.

"My bad. I never expected to see the two of you together and holding hands. So, this is how you do your best friend?" he asked Dawson directly, ignoring Riley.

Dawson let go of Riley's hand and stepped forward. His first thought was to know Roderick on his ass, but he held back the moment he felt Riley's hand touch his arm lightly.

"Correction number two for you tonight is I am

not your best friend. Best friends don't leave each other hanging and holding the bag for them."

"Okay, I'll give you that. I guess I should have said, my ex-fiancé and my ex-best friend. Is that better?" Roderick said flippantly.

"Call it whatever you like. Goodbye," Riley said, turning to leave while reaching for Dawson's hand so that they could get out of the restaurant before a scene ensued.

"Oh, wait, don't leave. Are you still angry after all of this time? All that is water under the bridge. I guess I'll be the bigger person and say it's good to see you both, though it's kind of turning my stomach at the moment to see you together. You know, for some reason, I'm not surprised. This is what you've always wanted, right Dawson? You've always had a thing for Riley and you were waiting for me to be out of the picture in order for you to make your move. Looks like you made it."

Dawson stopped and turned back, just when he thought he'd be able to walk away without things blowing up. Roderick was testing him and he wasn't having it.

"I didn't have to wait for anything and whatever is going on between me and Riley is none of your business. Looks like you have your own business going on at your table. Maybe you should get back to it, since this situation right here, is not about you," Dawson said.

"Please. She's not going anywhere. I'm too irresistible to resist," Roderick said, making reference to the woman who was patiently sitting at the table waiting for him.

Riley looked at the woman who look away shyly after Roderick's comment. Another doormat for him to walk over, she guessed.

"Leave it to you to embarrass yet another woman. Like I said, let it go because this business, is not your business," Dawson said and again, attempted to leave. Too bad Roderick continued to edge him on.

"Oh really? Were you seeing her behind my back the whole time we were engaged? I mean, I know you were in love with her, but really, you swoop in and make her yours?"

"I didn't have to make her mine after you took the cowards way out like you always do, leaving me to pick up the pieces for you."

Dawson was enraged with the nerve Roderick could muster up to throw shade his way.

"Oh, so this is you picking up the pieces for me? Should I say thank you now or later?" Roderick said snidely.

Dawson was losing patience and others in the restaurant were starting to notice the tension even though they weren't talking that loud.

"Let it go, Rod. You don't want this, trust me, you don't. Why are you back? Ruining someone else's life?" Dawson said, looking at the woman still sitting at the table where Roderick had been sitting, acting as if Roderick wasn't making a fool of himself and her.

"Dude, I enhance people's lives. She's just a friend. I came back for Riley because I missed her and she was the best thing to ever happen to me," Roderick admitted and then looked to Riley.

With a stunned look on her face after his admission, Riley looked to the woman sitting at the table and saw the humiliation on her face at being dismissed so easily by Roderick. It was clear she had a different opinion of what they were to each other. She then turned to him and addressed him directly.

"You didn't come for me after what you did. You must be out of your mind to think could even contemplate coming for me for anything."

"You loved me Riley and me getting cold feet happens. I'm sure we can talk about this and get beyond it. I've really missed you."

Riley laughed off his comment to keep from cursing him out. She had to give him credit for having balls big enough to pump himself up.

"You sicken me," she said. "I was gullible and you treated me like crap. I would never entertain that from anyone again."

Roderick looked at her and rubbed his chin.

"Let me get this straight. You can forgive this guy, but not me? He knew everything that I had been doing the whole time we were together, but he didn't tell you. He knew about all the women I cheated on you with. He knew all about Stacy and knew that I wasn't going to go through with the wedding," Roderick said.

"That's a lie!" Dawson shouted.

"Sure, you did. The night before the wedding at the bachelor party I told you that I was planning on marrying Stacy and you didn't say anything. Was that because you would rather see Riley crushed so that you could jump in and save the day? I guess by now you've told her about my three-year-old daughter, too. I see you're all lovey-dovey, but did you tell her all of my secrets that you helped me keep from her? You were a good friend to me, but what does that say about your feelings for Riley? You knew I wasn't going to show up, especially after Stacy showed up at the bachelor party and I left with her. I wish I could count the number of times you let me use your place to hook up with this woman or that one. Hey, I can honestly say I messed up and I'm sorry for that. I'm a changed man now and I want to try and make things right with Riley. Who would have known that you would slide in while I was gone?"

Riley was stunned. Roderick had a daughter who had been conceived by another woman while they were together and she knew nothing? Dawson knew and never said anything even after all hell broke loose at the church when Roderick didn't show up? Dawson knew the whole time of his deceit and didn't say anything? This was a man who said he loved her, but he kept those things from her? She turned to Dawson completely ignoring Roderick. His mess she dealt with because that was who Roderick was, but for Dawson to hold secrets from her?

"You knew all along that Roderick was messing around on me and you never told me? You knew he had a daughter during the time I was involved with and then engaged to him? After all this time, you still never told me? Why wouldn't you tell me about all of that? Even now with what we've shared, why wouldn't you tell me those things?"

Dawson didn't know who to be angry at – Riley for being naïve or Roderick for turning the tables and putting the blame on him.

"You're mad at me over the things he'd been doing? He's a grown man and it wasn't my place to tell you about any of it. That was your relationship with him."

They turned when Roderick broke out in laughter.

"Do I detect some problems going on here? You mean you didn't tell her about the role you played in all of this? You were right there helping me with excuses, coming in to save the day when I needed a way out of something. Dawson, always there to play the go-between role. He was Robin to my Batman!" Roderick laughed, proud of the mess that he was causing.

Everyone around them was now tuned into their discussion and Dawson was done entertaining them.

"Let's go, Riley," he said, ignoring Roderick.

When he looked at her, he saw her eyes glued on Roderick and his blood began to boil.

"I'm not leaving," she said curtly.

"That's right lover boy. She and I have some unfinished business to discuss. Looks like she's more pissed at you than at me. I may have done some cruel things, but at least I'm not the one who let her hurt and watched it play out without saying a word. We have history that goes back six years and whatever the two of you had, it can never compare to what she and I once had and can have again once we can sit down and talk."

"Talk?" Dawson questioned.

Roderick ignored him and turned his attention to Riley.

"Let me talk to you for a few minutes," he said.

"Riley?" Dawson said looking at her questionably.

"I can't believe you let me question everything about myself and all the while you helped him in his games. You saw how devastated I was the day of the wedding and you still didn't tell me the whole truth. How could you say you love me and you've kept things from me all this time?" she asked.

Roderick feigned choking, adding more drama to the scene as it played out.

"Love? He finally told you he was in love with you? He didn't tell you because he wanted you to be hurt so that you would be vulnerable and he could play on your emotional state. I loved you for six years and that should count for something even though I've hurt you. I've had counseling to deal with some issues I've had with commitment. I'm better and ready to do the right thing by you."

Dawson couldn't believe his ears or the fact that Riley was still standing in front of him listening to it all. What she should have been doing was hightailing it out of the restaurant and getting as far away from Roderick as she could get.

"You're saying all this with a woman sitting at the table, hurt and embarrassed by your confession of all the things you did to Riley. Then you admit how much you want her back," Dawson said.

As soon as they looked toward the table, the woman got up and headed toward the restroom.

"Give me five minutes, Riley, please. I know it's been a trying time, but if you give me a chance to explain everything, I think we can mend what was broken. I can tell you all about what I've been through and what counseling revealed that led me back to you," Roderick said, pleading.

Dawson didn't understand why Riley wasn't angrier at Roderick, but she appeared to be angry with him. He was done talking.

"Riley, are you leaving with me or staying?" he asked. When she didn't answer right away, he had his answer. "I guess I don't have to ask again," he said and walked away toward the door. What hurt even more was when he turned around, hoping to see Riley following him, but instead she stood talking to Roderick without even a glance his way. He guessed Riley was like many other women who didn't feel like they deserved to be loved better. He exited the restaurant, headed toward his car without looking back and realized he'd lost when he didn't even realize there was another person in the ring.

"Now, that we don't have Dawson as a distraction anymore, I hope you'll let me explain a few things. Come have a seat for a minute," Roderick said.

Riley was stunned that the night had turned out the way that it had. One minute she and Dawson were enjoying a fantastic night out and the next, her past walks up and destroys her joyful night.

"You're here with someone and this is her seat," she said.

"She's just a friend and when she returns, I'll give her money for a cab or something. The only thing important right now is you."

Riley didn't sit and she had no plans of doing so. She'd been waiting a long time to have her say and she was going to have it. Just as she was about to speak, the woman he had been sitting with returned to the table. She watched as Roderick reached for his wallet, no doubt about to hand the woman money for a cab as he said he would. Before he could, she invited the woman to sit back in her own seat.

"Please have a seat. I apologize for interrupting your evening right now, but this won't take long," she said and turned back to him. He spoke to the woman at the table before she could get a word out.

"Nonsense. Cynthia, I'm sorry about tonight. Riley and I have some things we need to talk through and I don't want you to sit here through all of this. Let me get you a cab to take you home."

As he reached for his wallet, Riley stood stunned that he had the gall to treat this woman like this in her presence. He was slime. She should have known it back then, but now she does. She was seeing clearer than she ever had.

"Really, Roderick? You changed? Isn't that what you said? What kind of man does this to a woman? You brought her here tonight and I'm thinking, by her reaction to all of this, that she's more than a friend and your answer is to put her in a cab?"

"Well, you stayed to talk to me and Dawson left. You know you still love me and I still love you. We need to talk about this while it's still fresh," he pleaded.

"Fresh? This isn't fresh for me. It's dead, buried and now stinking up the place. We don't have anything to talk about. I'm going to talk and you're going to listen. What you did to me was horrible, deplorable, inexcusable and unforgiveable."

"Baby, you don't mean that," he said, interrupting her.

Riley's anger went to a whole new level.

"Don't call me baby and I mean every single word

of it. You don't get to think and speak for me. I'm quite capable of doing that myself. You left me at the church on our wedding day to explain to all of my family that there would be no wedding. Somehow, your family didn't show up and I should have found that odd when I arrived at the church and was told no one on your side was in attendance. Still, I waited two hours and no Roderick. You didn't even have the decency to answer the phone any of the hundreds of times that I called you. You did seem to find time to call Dawson to tell him to break the news to me. Did you and Dawson think this was some teenage game? That was my life you played with and it turned into the most embarrassing moment that I have ever experienced."

"Riley, I'm trying to apologize."

"Shut up! I'm talking now," she screamed, drawing the attention of everyone in the restaurant. She didn't care. She had waited a long time to get these thoughts off of her and she wasn't leaving until she did.

Roderick looked around.

"Keep your voice down," he said. "You're drawing attention to yourself."

"What? Does the attention embarrass you? Now you know how it feels. You have no idea how hard that day and the days following it were. Did you even care? Now, here you are returning thinking you can pick things up with me as if you didn't ruin my life. You broke my heart and left me in financial debt. What happened? Did Stacy finally see you for who you really are? You think I want that back in my life? You make me sick. I'm just glad I have the chance to tell you how horrible a person I think you are and if I ever see you again, it will be too soon. I hope you enjoyed your dinner because the rest of it is on you."

Before she could second guess herself, Riley pulled the table cloth and dumped the meal from his plate and from the woman's plate right onto his lap. She stood back when Roderick stood as food fell from his shirt and lap to the floor.

She smiled at herself at how good it felt to finally put a snake in the grass in his place. She looked from him to the woman who now appeared to be as angry as she was. Knowing how pitiful the woman probably felt, Riley wanted her to have a little satisfaction from the night. She reached to the table behind her, grabbed a glass of water and handed it to the woman. Without saying a word, the woman threw the glass of water in Roderick's face. When Riley turned to leave, she saw the woman stand, too.

Girl power, she thought as she left, holding her head up knowing that over a year ago, she escaped the biggest mistake of her life.

11

Riley drove down Dawson's street for the fifth time trying to build up the nerve to get out and knock on the door. For the past week, she'd thought of nothing other than seeing him. They hadn't spoken since that night at the restaurant when they ran into Roderick.

That night was a turning point for her. After telling Roderick what she really thought and finally getting the closure she needed, she felt like a new woman. As she left the restaurant, it was like a major weight had been lifted. She saw herself in a new light, she let go of the past that had plagued her for over a year and she realized nothing was more important to her than Dawson and his love.

For months, she'd taken him for granted and watched as he patiently stood on the side as she went through ups and downs. Seeing Roderick again brought back memories that made her temporarily forget about Dawson and what she really felt for him, but had been unable to express.

Her blood had been boiling at the sight of and listening to all of Roderick's arrogance, thinking that she would take him back after the horrible way he'd treated her. She never was or would be that desperate for any man. Dawson was a different story. She was desperate for him. She had been angry with him that night, but not enough to make her walk away from him – not ever again. Deep down, she knew it wasn't him who needed to tell her about Roderick and all of his secrets. He did those things right in front of her face and she never knew and she should have. Back then, she had been blinded by what she thought was love for him. Now all she harbored was disgust and pity.

Dawson, on the other hand, was everything to her and she was sorry it took her all this time to really understand what it felt like to really be loved unconditionally by a man. The day he walked out of the restaurant, she could see how hurt he really and finally was. He hadn't reached out since then and she didn't want him to. It was time she did the reaching and fixing their relationship – that is if he was still open to having one with her. Like he always confessed to her, she wasn't leaving and would always be there for him if he allowed her to. She loved him and nothing was going to get in the way of finally telling him that. He'd been in her corner more than once encouraging and comforting her even when she was down on herself.

She was glad that this time, after encountering Roderick, she didn't crawl back into her place of isolation and loneliness. She no longer felt the need to do that. She knew her life was better and happier Dawson in it and she was miserable without him.

A smarter woman wouldn't let a good man like Dawson wait and wait for them to get their act together. He was more than patient and she didn't show him the same level of patience and love.

Pulling closer to his house, she decided to get out this time and claim the man who had won her heart. Stopping and turning her car off, she sat for a minute looking at the car in his driveway. It wasn't a car she recognized. She wondered if he'd already moved on. Even though it had only been a week, women threw themselves at him all the time. She's seen many second and third glances by women when they were out someplace together. There was no doubt he was as sexy as they come and even more so naked, but it was everything about him that she loved. The naked part had been a bonus. It was now or never, she thought.

"No time to question yourself. You don't let a good man like Dawson get away," she said to herself before getting out and walking with confidence to the door. For this visit, she wouldn't use her code, not knowing if he'd reprogrammed it to no longer give her access. She rang the bell and nervously waited.

"Riley?" Dawson questioned, surprised to see her standing on the other side of the door. As angry as she'd been with him, he figured she'd never speak to him again and yet, here she was at his door.

"Hi. I know you weren't expecting me and I hope I'm not interrupting anything," she said looking past him at the beautiful woman walking up to them from inside of his house. She watched as Dawson looked from her to the other woman. Insecurity began creeping in. "Maybe I should leave. I'm sorry for popping up like this especially after the way I talked to you last week and it looks like you're busy," she said and turned to walk away.

"Wait," the woman said.

Riley stopped at the sound of the woman's voice.

"Riley, don't leave," Dawson said.

When she looked at him, all she saw was love and it washed over her like a warm embrace.

"I was just leaving and I'm sure the two of you need to talk. I'm Mia, Dawson's sister, well half-sister. I was actually on my way out when you arrived, so this is a great time to make my exit." Mia turned to Dawson. "Don't forget what I said." After giving him one last hug, she walked around Riley.

"Come in," Dawson said.

Feeling like a fool over her immediate jealousy the moment she saw the woman in his house, Riley walked inside with her head down before turning to face him.

"So, that was your other sister, huh? The one you're always raving about that I had never met?" she asked, hoping to lighten up the extremely tense moment they were having.

"Yes, she came by to tell me she passed the bar on her first try. She's in town to visit our father and decided to see me while she was here. I assumed I wouldn't see you again after what happened," he said.

"What? You thought I would be in Roderick's arms again?"

"I didn't know what to think. You seemed angrier at me than you were at him and I assumed his hurt was worse than mine."

Riley knew his words couldn't be further from the truth.

"True. I can see how you might think that, but you left out of there so fast, you didn't stick around for the show."

Dawson smiled. He didn't want to say how happy he was to see her because in his mind, what had started developing between them was over.

"There was a show?" he asked.

"I'll tell you about it if we don't have to stand here at the door as if any minute, you're going to throw me out."

When Dawson laughed out loud, she laughed too, happy that they could laugh together even though the moment should have felt uncomfortable.

"Come on into the kitchen. I was cleaning up."

"Did you have a party or something? That's a lot of dishes," she said.

"My mother and sister were here last night and they ended up cooking what could amount to a mini feast. I volunteered to clean up and didn't feel like doing it last night."

After loading the last dishes and turning on the washer, Dawson turned around and leaned back against the sink.

"What brings you to my part of town?" he asked.

Now or never, Riley thought.

"I missed you," she said quickly with confidence.

"You missed me? Are you sure?" he asked, crossing his arms across his chest.

"Yes, I'm sure."

"Tell me about this show I missed after I left the restaurant," he said. If he had known there would be a show, he would have stayed around. What he didn't want to see was Riley forget about the slime ball she finally discovered Roderick turned out to be and go running back to him. He knew Roderick would never change and he wasn't the man for Riley. The only man for her was him.

"Well, Roderick begged me to forgive him. Instead, I finally got the chance to say all of the things I'd been holding in for a year about what a horrible person he was and still is. I unloaded on him and it felt good! Then I swiped the entire contents of the table, especially the food, in his lap. The best part was he said all of this while his date sat there like a lump of clay listening to him say how much he still loved me. He's so arrogant that he couldn't see why a woman wouldn't want him. I think I knew all along what he was about, but never did I think that he would treat a woman like that to her face. While he stood shocked at what I did, I handed her a glass from the neighboring table and she through the contents into his face. I actually gave her a lift home and she thanked me for revealing who he really was before she got too involved. I wish I could describe how good it felt to finally tell him off. I never got the chance to do that after he walked out on me, but now it's all finally behind me. I really needed to do that and I hope you understand," she said and looked at him for any sign that he understood what she needed to do.

"You did what? I wish I had stuck around for that. I'm sure Roderick was a sight to see. I do understand. How are you now?" he asked.

Riley smiled. With everything, he was still concerned about her.

"That is you, isn't it? You are that person who really cares about another person's feelings and I didn't see it. I mean, I know I saw it and I felt it, but I didn't acknowledge it like I should have. For a year, I whined and cried about how Roderick did this and that to me and not once did you rat him out, something that would have put you in a better light with me. You knew that and still you didn't tell me the extent of his deceit."

"I didn't want you that way. I wanted you to want

me for how I loved and treated you, not because of how bad he treated you. All of those things he confessed he had done, I could have told you and you probably would not have suffered for a year wondering if the breakup was your fault. You would have gotten over it and come to me as some type of hero because I pointed out his faults and thereby, pumping up myself to you. I didn't want you like that.

"Was Roderick, right? Have you been in love with me for a long time?" she asked.

No need to hesitate, Dawson thought. Now was the time to put it all out in the open.

"Yes, even while you were dating and then engaged to him. I saw you for who you were and I saw him, too. He wasn't worthy of the incredible woman you are."

"You never said anything before this year."

"I couldn't. You were in love with Roderick and prepared to marry him. It was what you wanted and it wasn't my place to step in the middle of that. To me, you were happy. I didn't like it, but you were. I knew all of the things he'd been doing and it made me sick to know that you didn't have a clue. Times when I tried to tell him how wrong he was and question how he could treat a good woman like you that way, he would laugh it off and say that I was jealous because I wanted you. He was a jerk and always had been. He was the brother I didn't have growing up and when we became friends, it was because we had love for playing baseball. I did what brothers do and I kept his secrets. After he met you, I knew from the start that you weren't for him – not because you weren't good enough, but because I knew he wasn't good enough for you."

So many things began to click for Riley as she thought back to when she was with Roderick.

"That night two years ago at the party that girl name Rachel he worked with had when you gave me a ride home because Roderick didn't show up, you told me then that I could do better than him. You knew where he was?" she asked.

"I did. He was with Stacy and sent me a text telling me to look after you and keep the guys away from you. That was the only reason I stayed around for the entire night. I knew you didn't really know anyone there and I didn't want you to feel isolated. I didn't give a damn about his request. I didn't want you to feel alone in a room full of people you didn't know."

"I was so blind that I never suspected he was a cheating philanderer and he has a kid? That, I think I did know about. There were signs and once while out with him, someone congratulated him on the baby. He whisked me away real fast and when I asked, he said the guy got him mixed up with someone else at his office. I never would have put up with any of that had I known. It would have ended way before he left me standing at the church on our wedding. Instead, I had to hear from you that he wasn't coming and that he was already in Aruba with Stacy. Did you know that he was going to do that? Leave me on our wedding day?" she asked.

Dawson came around the counter, took her hands in his and looked her in the eyes.

"That was something I knew nothing about or I never would have let it get that far. I didn't find out until I got that text from him. I tried calling him several times, but he'd turned his phone off. I paced for thirty minutes trying to figure out what to do until I went to your mother and told her what he'd done. She wanted to kill him and I convinced her to let me tell you. I felt all of the blame because he had been messing up for a long time and if I had told you, that embarrassing day never would have happened. I'm sorry for that."

Riley reached a hand up and caressed his face.

"You don't have to apologize for a situation that was not of your making. That was all Roderick and I want you to know that I am over that. Last week, I finally got the closure I needed and I'm over it. I've been over him for a long time, but the residue of the situation was like a piece of gum on the bottom of your shoe that you can't seem to get off. It's there irritating you and you hope it will dissolve and go away, but it doesn't."

"What does that mean for us? Are we good? Am I back in the friend zone?" he asked.

"Friend zone? Oh, hell no. There is no more friend zone for you!" she declared and tried to hold a steady, straight face with no emotion showing.

"What?" Dawson asked.

Was he hearing that she didn't want him either and not even as a friend?

"You heard me. No friend zone for you because like you, I love you and there's no going back to just being friends for us. I love you," she said again and exaggerated the word love to make sure he understood the meaning.

"Wait – what? Did you really just say that you love me? Are you sure?"

"Oh, it's not just loving you, I'm in love with you and I have been for a while. I doubted myself so much that I couldn't bring myself to say what I had been feeling. There is no more doubt. I love you."

Dawson smile. "Those words are music to my ears and you're sure that you're sure," he said grinning from ear to ear.

Riley raised her other hand to use both to caress his face and hold it in place as she pulled him closer to her.

"You have no idea how sure I am," she said.

Without the need for any more words, she kissed him sweetly while keeping her eyes on him. The moment he joined her in the kiss and deepened it, she closed her eyes and felt herself being swept up into a moment that romance novels were famous for. She let her arms drop down around his shoulders and the moment she felt his hands grasp her hips, turning her all the way around to face him, she knew that the kiss was sealing a love that was meant to be. While she'd wasted her time on a creep, a real, good man was right in the wings waiting for her to come to her senses.

Pulling back, Riley looked into the eyes of the man she truly loved.

"I love you," Dawson said.

"And I love you. I'm sorry it took me this long to tell you because I've felt this way for a few months now. I wasn't sure it was right to feel that way. Now, I know that love wants who and what it wants and love wanted us to love each other."

"Baby, you deserve nothing, but the greatest love any man can give a woman. I promise you will always feel safe and secure with me and in my arms; always."

Leaning down and pulling Riley even closer, Dawson embraced his love and kissed her lips softly, meaning every word of it. He'd waited what seemed an eternity for Riley and his love for her was going to be forever.

"I've never met a man as wonderful as you and I'll never take you or your love for granted ever again. I'm ready for what's in store for us. I love you, I love you!" she declared.

"I love you, too, baby," Dawson said, kissing her sweetly to prove he was all in with her.

To show how all in she was with him, Riley began

unbuttoning her top, while looking up at him with a sexy grin, the kind that said everything she had on her mind. To say she was hungry for all of him would be an understatement.

"I love you and I want you. I've thought of nothing, but being in your arms again and again. I've never felt that way before and I know I never will again unless it's with you. Make love to me. I want and need to feel you" she uttered rapturously.

"Are you sure? The last time we did that, I woke up and you were gone."

"Trust me, that will never, ever happen again. There is no place I'd rather be than in love, loving you and having you love me over and over again."

Dawson laughed.

"Do I need to handcuff you to my bed this time to keep you from disappearing with only a sad note left behind?" he asked.

"*Mmm*, you have handcuffs? Can I use them on you?"

"Woman, don't get me started!" Dawson said ardently.

"Well, do you still want me?" she asked.

"I never stopped wanting you."

"Show me," Riley said and waited for him to make a move.

When he did, her life was finally right-side-up. How she ever came close to not having him was beyond her. This is the kind of man and love all women long for. She would never again question his true heart when it came to her. He wore it open and honest on his sleeve. She's just happy that she focused enough to see it and see him for who he was. She looked at her love and anticipated what was coming next. It could only be something good and delicious!

12

Dawson's first thought was to pick Riley up and take her upstairs to his bedroom, but for the life of him, he couldn't get his mind focused on where his bedroom was. The only thing he could think about was taking her up on her offer for him to show her how much he really wanted her.

After that night at the restaurant, he never thought he'd get the chance to show her again. He wasn't going to mess it up by fumbling this moment. Before she could say another word, he leaned down and kissed her deeply letting her know he remembered how she liked to be kissed. It was a prelude to what was to come. Devouring her mouth, he poured everything about his love for her into the kiss that turned wild as they went at each other's mouths like two starving animals. The kiss was passionate and intense and there was no doubt that they loved each other. This wasn't a game, he thought.

He pulled back and looked her in the eyes, trying to send her a wordless message that his love was never-ending and she was more than enough for him.

"I'm all yours," she said, seductively.

"That's good because I plan to have you, all of you for as long as you'll allow me."

He reached down and pulled his tank top out of the top of his jeans and pulled it over his head. He smiled at the intake of breath Riley took in as her gaze took in his chest only a breath away.

"Yes!" she said with an excitement she pulled from deep down. This is what she'd wanted since their first time.

"All yours, baby," he said and reached for her sweater to pull it up and off of her body. After tossing it to the counter behind them, unsnap and remove her bra. As if fell from her body, he let it drop to the floor as he leaned down and took one of her pebbled nipples into his mouth, rolling his tongue back and forth across first one then the other, smiling when she emitted a whimper. He loved her breasts and he was hungry to have them in his mouth, encased in his wide hands and rubbing against his chest as they engaged in carnality that took them to a higher plane. Already, he could feel the heat emanating from her body and his body reacted by going hard in an instant.

Placing his hands on either side of her on the countertop, he dropped his head down as he felt her hands reach for his belt and slowly unzipped his pants. He felt his heart rate speed up with anxiety unable to focus because his desire for her was unimaginable. He wanted to participate in removing his clothes, but he was hypnotized by the fact that this was Riley, a woman he loved more than anything and she finally came to him and wanted him just for him. He wanted to touch her, to kiss her, to feel her writhe underneath of him as he whispered in her ear sweet subtleties. He'd never felt this kind of love or lust before.

When he thought he couldn't possibly get more excited than he already was, he felt weak in the knees the moment she pushed his jeans and boxers down his legs. When she couldn't get them any further down beyond his knees, he almost leaped out of them when she reached up and stroked his already rock-hard penis with both of her hands. He thought he'd died and gone to heaven the moment she leaned forward to place kisses across his chest. Kicking his clothes from his legs, he didn't think he could wait another second before being inside of her.

Capturing her lips again, he reached under her skirt until he encountered the thin strap of the thong she was hiding under her long, flowing skirt. When she lifted her hips slightly, he slid the thong down her legs and off to the floor. With no barrier between them, he lifted her from the stool, braced her legs around his taut waist and walked to the closest smooth surface, the wall on the other side of the kitchen entrance.

Holding her up with one hand under her behind, Dawson used the other to guide himself into her body and leaned his head on her shoulder the moment he felt the heat of the inside of her body surround him.

"I'm yours. Nothing can stop this love," Riley said as she moved up and down on him. The feel of him was magnificent and everything she remembered him being from their first time. She hadn't imagined how long and thick he was and it wasn't a one-time thing. His member was a beast and it was beating her into submission and she loved it. As he increased the pace, she held on tight as her body tingled and shivered with amorous delight. She moved around on him in circles and then moved up and down, switching between the two, noticing how much he loved her movements.

"That's it, baby. Take what you want because everything I am is for you," Dawson groaned out as he surged into her body, giving her all of him.

Bracing his feet on the floor and one hand planted firmly on the wall, he loved her while at the same time accepting her love in return. To him this was the beginning of the best kind of love. To him there was nothing better than loving a black woman. They loved from a place deep down in their souls and when they loved you, they loved you forever as long as they felt loved and needed. As he made love to Riley vigorously, he poured all of his love into his lovemaking making sure she would never have a doubt of his commitment to her and to their love. Black love was incredible.

As he felt Riley grip him with her inner muscles, he knew that she was close and he wanted to feel her come apart in his arms. He wanted to feel her love flow from her body and cover every part of his.

"I'm there, Dawson!" Riley screamed.

Surging deeper and harder, he gave her everything he had and the moment she screamed his name and came with a force, he followed her over the edge into a sexual bliss that he'd only been able to discover with her. The force of his orgasm hit him again and again until what seemed like rockets shot off in his head as the sheer magnitude of the explosion ripped through him. He continued to move inside of her until their breathing returned to normal and their bodies were covered with a thin sheen of sweat.

Dawson held them up on legs that were weak from their loving. He kissed Riley passionately, loving the feel and the taste of her. Her taste branded him as hers and he needed her taste as much as he needed to breath.

"You are amazing," he said the moment he could form words again.

"So are you and when you show me, you really show me!" Riley exclaimed.

"Can I show you even more in my bed?" he asked.

"Well, you'll have to carry me because I'm not

sure my legs will work enough for me to walk there on my own."

"I got you, baby," he said. "Now, if we happen to fall to the floor on our way, then the next time will be on the floor," he quipped.

"Floor, bed anywhere as long as I get to always feel you like this."

Dawson finally had his love where he wanted her and she was all his. He would always remember the wait knowing she was well worth it. Her heart was huge, her love embraced him and together, they would be the epitome of what it meant to love unconditionally. That's how black love was created, he thought.

"Now and forever. My love for you is real and it's everlasting and I never, ever want you to doubt that."

Riley knew any doubt she had had already flown the coop.

"I now know what real love is and it's all I need," she said.

"Let's find a bed and discover even more of it. The night is young and this time when you fall asleep in my arms, I want to wake up make love to you again and then again and then again. Thank you for choosing my love over not having love at all."

Riley kissed him.

"Thank you for never giving up on the love you have for me."

Riley jumped when she felt Dawson's hands travel

down her body while she felt him grow hard and long again while still buried deep inside of her.

Dawson grinned knowing why.

"Problem?" he asked.

"A bed, right now!" she exclaimed while wiggling her hips around on him.

"The bed gets my vote! I hope you don't have any place to go later or tomorrow because I'm planning on holding you hostage for a few days."

Dawson lifted her and carried her up the stairs, not breaking their intimate contact.

"You know I'm never letting you go."

Riley held on tight to his shoulders.

"I'd never let you because this love is forever."

More exciting romance from Cheryl Barton
Get books 1 – 4 of the Bachelor Series

Book 1 – "Bachelor Not for Sale"

Even self-proclaimed "bachelors for life" meet that one woman that makes them want to slow down and second guess bachelorhood. After suffering through the heartache of what he thought was true love, Duron Knight meets and becomes enchanted with bombshell Taija Charles.

Taija has heard a lot about Duron and all of her body senses are on overdrive when she meets the handsome bachelor face to face. As the sparks fly, Taija plans to show Duron how she can help him mend his broken heart with real love and the right amount of lust.

Book 2 – "A Designed Affair"

In the follow-up to "Bachelor Not for Sale", Loren Knight has been engaging in a secret love affair with her brother Duron's best friend and business partner, Michael Bailey. He is everything she could want and more in a man, but she believes the risk is too great for any type of relationship with him beyond the bedroom door.

Michael Bailey has been fighting his attraction to Loren for years. He has stayed away from her out of respect for his best friend and business partner. Now that he and Loren have finally given into passion that they both have been craving, can Michael convince Loren that what they share is worth the risk?

Book 3 – "A Perfect Combination

In the third installment following "Bachelor Not for Sale" and "A Designed Affair", Tyrone Davis is the king of one-night-stands; nicknamed, Mr. Love Them and Leave Them. He learned to perfect it from his two best friends, Duron Knight and Michael Bailey. He never imagined a one-night stand would have such a lasting impact, but that's exactly what happened.

Victoria Alston couldn't forget the incredible night she spent with Tyrone Davis, someone connected to one of her best friends. The next day, she disappeared, returning to reality and the fiancé she'd left in Boston while on business travel. They both soon discovered that it wasn't just a one-night stand, but a perfect combination for love.

Book 4 – "Love at Last"

In the third follow-up to "Bachelor Not for Sale", they had the perfect love...That's what Brian Knight thought of his relationship with Sherry Braxton until he looked up one day and she was gone and never wanted to see him again. Two years later, he discovered that there is the possibility that Sherry may have been pregnant with his child. Hurt and angry at her deceit, he takes a flight to Baltimore to fight for his rights as a father and realizes that the love and passion they once shared had never died. Is it possible he could still have the kind of love he thought would last a lifetime? Can he still have his love at last?

Un-Break My Heart

Dr. Mackenzie Ellis suffered a loss so great, she never thought she'd fall in love again, especially with someone close to her.

Travis Blackwell, III never dreamed of crossing the line with Mackenzie until his heart would no longer allow him to deny the love he has for her and the passion he wants to share with her knowing that he is the key to mending her broken heart.

Bossy

Cassidy 'Bossy' Bostic came from nothing, but knew she would be something. Pregnant and alone, she was forced to run from her past in order to have a future. Her rise to the top as the owner of a fashion dynasty is what dreams are made of, but her hard, icy persona could have her living a lonely existence.

Drake Montgomery, a rising attorney heading toward the political arena, has fallen in love with the 'Bossy' mogul only to discover it's 'Cassidy' he loves, but 'Bossy', not so much.

Can their hot, steamy romance melt even her cold, icy heart? Only time and love will tell.

Heartthrob

Cade Weston, Hollywood's most eligible bachelor and named the world's sexiest man of the year, lives life at the top with a bevy of beauties at his beck and call, people providing his every desire and more money than any one person should have.

Callie Hurston struggles to make it as a stylist to the stars in a world where women are intimidated by her beauty and men are interested in her body and not her talent.

Cade thought he had it all until he has a chance meeting with Callie and decides to take a chance on her talent and ends up taking an even bigger chance with his heart.

Can the playboy turn in his player's card and give in to love?

His Halloween Promise

Dylan Kennedy and Savannah Eaton-Kennedy may be divorced, but that doesn't stop them from indulging in some pretty hot and sexy encounters.

A divorce decree may mean that their life together is over, but Dylan has a promise to keep that could bring his wife back where she belongs; in his life, permanently.

Home for Thanksgiving

Firefighter Nicholas Sullivan is going home for the holiday after he was sidelined due to an injury on the job. Guilt over a life lost has kept him away from his family's ranch in Montana and now he's forced to face his past demons and deal with a self-imposed life of regret.

Veterinarian Parker Wingate's first encounter with the handsome firefighter was less than pleasurable. She sympathized with his hurt, understood his pain and before long, felt his love.

Knowing the holiday season is ending soon, can Nick go from living in love for the moment to allowing himself to finally live in love forever?

A Better Man

Phoenix Graham is living her best life with the best man, her fiancé, Carson Stone, heir to the Stone Tower Hotel Empire. Her perfect life is shaken up when a handsome, rugged and extremely sexy mysterious man moves in across the hall and she begins to see that the rose-colored glasses she had been seeing life through were blinders. She soon discovers that Carson was the best man for her until she takes notice of a better man and his name is Gavin Black.

What's a girl to do when the best doesn't get better and better is what she craves?

Book 5 of the "Amorous Occupations" series
The Electrician

The party invitation said everyone had to wear a masquerade mask the entire night, a New Orleans tradition. Dara Marshall couldn't resist the opportunity to spend an uninhibited night of passion with National Football Association coach Nelson Riley, the guest of honor, knowing that her identity was hidden by her mask.

Dara's world turns upside down when she discovers the gorgeous coach is the newest client of her father's business and after she's sent on a job at his condo, she does everything in her power to not give away the secret of who she is.

Nelson could never forget the sexy temptress he'd spent an unforgettable night with, even when she tries to hide behind a mask and baggy overalls.

Love on Top

Brandon and Dakota King's love was like a fairytale from the start and then a level of comfort set in and Brandon's priority became his ambition for bigger, more and greater when it came to business. Dakota began losing patience when it appears love was no longer a priority to him.

When Brandon realized he had been taking love for granted, he puts a plan in place to prove to his wife that he values "Love on Top" over everything else. His dilemma? Is it too late?

About the Author

Cheryl Barton lives in Maryland and in her spare time she loves to read espionage novels, cook, watch Sci-fi movies, spend time with family and friends and enjoy Maryland steamed crabs.

I am because you read and I thank you! - Cheryl

Connect with me

Visit my website at www.cherylbarton.net for copies of all novels.

www.ingramcontent.com/pod-product-compliance
Lightning Source LLC
Chambersburg PA
CBHW050825180626
46814CB00004B/1460